MW01136268

Ladies of the Sky

Ladies of the Sky

Sadie's Shadow

Ladies of the Sky #1

by

Julia Mills

Once You Take Flight,

the World Will Never Look the Same

Again.

ACKNOWLEDGEMENTS

Edited by Lisa Miller, Angel Editing Services

Proofread by Tammy Payne with Book Nook Nuts

Cover Designed by Linda Boulanger with Tell Tale Book Covers

Formatted by Charlene Bauer with Wickedly Bold Creations

DEDICATION

Dare to Dream! Find the Strength to Act! Never Look Back!

Thank you, God.

To my girls, Liz and Em, I Love You. Every day, every way, always.

Gaelic as Spoken by Dragon Kin

Sadie's Shadow

Banphrionsa beag………. Little princess

Máthair………. Mother

Athair………. Father

Soith olc………. Evil bitch

Mianach………. Mine

Sianach deirfiúr………. Sister mine

Deirfiúr………. Sister

Mo dragoness…….My dragoness

Mo banphrionsa………My princess

Tá tú mianach………. You are mine

Tá mé mise………I am yours

Bbeo fada, grá maith agus ag eitilt ard………. Live long, love well and fly high

Mo stór………My treasure

Mo dragoness álainn.......... My beautiful dragoness

Grá mo chroí.......... Love of my heart

Le grá go deo, gráim thú.......... With love fore, I love you.

Mo bhanríon.......... My queen

Mo rí.......... My king

Beidh mé grá duít go geo.......... I will always love you

Is brae liom tú.......... I love you

Japanese as spoken by the Golden Dragons of Tokyo

Sadie's Shadow

U~izādo....... Wizards

Hai.......... Yes

Arigatōgozaimashita.......... Thank you

Masutādoragon.........Master Dragon

Dōhō.......... Brethren

Meiyo no shakkin.......... Debt of Honor

Sayōnara.......... Goodbye

Also by Julia Mills

*****

The Dragon Guard Series

Her Dragon to Slay, Dragon Guard #1

Her Dragon's Fire, Dragon Guard #2

Haunted by Her Dragon, Dragon Guard #3

For the Love of Her Dragon, Dragon Guard #4

Saved by Her Dragon, Dragon Guard #5

Only for Her Dragon, Dragon Guard #6

Fighting for Her Dragon, Dragon Guard #7

Her Dragon's Heart, Dragon Guard #8

Her Dragon's Soul, Dragon Guard #9

The Fate of Her Dragon, Dragon Guard #10

Her Dragon's No Angel, Dragon Guard #11

Her Dragon, His Demon, Dragon Guard #12

Resurrecting Her Dragon, Dragon Guard #13

The Scars of Her Dragon, Dragon Guard #14

Ladies of the Sky

Her Mad Dragon, Dragon Guard #15

Tears for Her Dragon, Dragon Guard #16

Guarding Her Dragon, Dragon Guard #17

Sassing Her Dragon, Dragon Guard #18 (Sassy Ever After Kindle World)

Kiss of Her Dragon, Dragon Guard #19

Claws, Class and a Whole Lotta Sass, Dragon Guard #20 (Sassy Ever After Kindle World)

The Dragon with the Girl Tattoo, Dragon Guard #21 (Paranormal Dating Agency Kindle World)

Her Love, Her Dragon: The Saga Begins, A Dragon Guard Prequel

*****

The 'Not-Quite' Love Story Series

Vidalia: A 'Not-Quite Vampire Love Story

Phoebe" A 'Not-Quite' Phoenix Love Story

Zoey: A 'Not-Quite' Zombie Love Story

Jax: A 'Not-Quite' Puma Love Story

Heidi: A 'Not-Quite' Hellhound Love Story (Magic & Mayhem
Kindle World)

Lola: A 'Not-Quite' Witchy Love Story (Magic & Mayhem
Kindle World)

*****

Kings of the Blood

VIKTOR: Heart of Her King ~ Kings of the Blood ~ Book 1

ROMAN: Fury of Her King ~ Kings of the Blood ~ Book2

ACHILLES: Soul of Her King ~ Kings of the Blood ~ Book 3

Ladies of the Sky

Chapter One

"Let me out of here!" His deep baritone echoed off the stone of the cave and roared through the forest, making the hairs on the back of the princess's neck stand on end and her stomach do flip-flops. "This will not stand. My brethren will find me. You will pay!" This was the third straight day he'd been issuing threats. Sadie almost wished he was still unconscious.

Almost…

"Our *guest* still issuing threats?" Phryne asked, sitting down beside the dragoness and dropping a pack full of supplies. "You really do need to decide what you're going to do with him." The Pegasus shifter poked Sadie's campfire with a stick, making sparks fly and fill the air between them before floating toward the Heavens.

Wish I could float away with them…

"The others are beginning to ask where you keep running off to. I'm not going to be able to keep them from coming to look for you for much longer; especially Gwendolyn. You know how she gets."

Blowing out a long-suffering sigh, Sadie could only nod and watch the flames eat away at the timber she had chopped earlier that day. Gwendolyn's persistence was legendary—it went past stubborn to obstinate—and irritated every single person in their small clan to near distraction. However, no one complained because it had saved them all more times than anyone could remember. Some said it was because she was a Thunderbird who had been raised without her parents or any kin of her kind, forced to deal with the oddities of her powers without proper guidance, but Sadie refused to accept that excuse. They had all been stolen from their families, packs, and clans by hunters, left to die on a snowy mountain, only alive by the grace of the Heavens and the loving hand of the Guardian. In some ways, they were stronger for it.

"Yes, I am aware."

"Have you checked his wounds today?" Phryne asked. "After all, you did put an arrow in his *hindquarters*." She made air quotes before bursting out laughing, making Sadie regret all the interactions with the humans her clan had experienced over the last twenty years. It had taken the others nearly a decade after the death of the Guardian to convince the princess that they needed to interact with humans, other supernatural beings, and the world at large, but on days like this one, she still doubted her decision.

"First of all, I was shooting at a deer. The buck was in my sights and I thought I was completely alone in the forest. I had scented, tested the surroundings with my preternatural senses, and even touched the mind of the animal. I would've bet money that I was alone with my prey. The arrow was already flying through the air and that…that *man* appeared out of thin air."

She still could not explain where he had come from. There was something about him that felt strange. Just being near him made both Sadie and her dragon uneasy, on edge, *irritable*, but they still craved his deep woody musk and his low rumbling voice, even when he was yelling and screaming.

"So, you still haven't answered my question." Phryne's voice held the hint of the chuckle she was trying to hide, dancing on Sadie's nerves like a jackhammer on concrete.

"He is healed," she ground out through gritted teeth. "I told you that yesterday when you asked and the day before that and the day before. You know as well as I do that he is also a dragon and can heal himself very quickly. Probably one of the Enforcers the Guardian told about all those years ago. Their story was sad and their fate unknown. That's the only explanation I can think of for his condition when we found him."

Holding up her hand as her sister-of-her-heart, sporting a sly grin and a twinkle in her eye, opened her mouth to speak, the

Leader of the Ladies of the Sky clan, as they had named themselves almost a century ago, continued, "My arrow was a small wound compared to his emaciated, skeletal appearance, the dirt, blood, and gore caked in his long hair and beard, and the cuts on his hands and feet."

Her smile fading, the winged-horse shifter bit her bottom lip before adding, "And those oozing wounds and scars. They had to have been from silver. Nothing else could harm the flesh of any shifter, especially one with magic as strong as his, in such a way."

"I know and I still cannot fathom the glyphs on his back. They had to have been carved into his skin and silver repeatedly added to the open cuts to make them permanent with such definition." She played with the thin braids that hung over her shoulder as she thought. "I need to see some of Laurel's books. She has all the old writings from the chapels in France. If anyone took note of something like we are seeing, it was the monks." Sadie opened the pack, looking for something to eat, and pulled out a ham sandwich. Focusing on what her sister was saying while trying to drown out the bellowing of the male dragon presently locked in their empty dry storage cavern, the dragoness unwrapped what was to be her dinner and took a bite.

"Good luck with that. She's as bad as you are about sharing her treasures. I guess it is true that gargoyles are like dragons when it comes to what they value most," Phryne said.

It was an old joke amongst their small clan, one that always ended with Laurel telling the Legend of the Gargouille, explaining how the first gargoyle sprang from the remains of a fallen dragon in seventh century France. But then that was how things had been for the seven of them since they had found themselves lost and alone in the care of the Guardian; a rag-tag group of female shifters with no family, no clan…no home. The girls had learned early that life is what you make it. They were fighters, each and every one of them, sisters-of-the heart that would defend their adopted family to death and beyond.

"Let me out of here *now*! I demand it!" their *patient* roared again. Sadie rolled her eyes and focused on her food, thinking about the past and how happy they had been for over a century keeping to the outskirts of society, protecting what was theirs, avoiding conflict…avoiding *others*.

One of her first memories of the Guardian and what would soon become her Destiny swirled through her mind, demanding her attention, blocking out even the screams of the man she feared could and *would* change her life forever…

"But where are my parents?"

19

The Guardian's naturally husky voice and calming nature filled the room as Sadie watched her cover one of the other girls with a thick woolen coverlet. "They are fighting the Great Evil, little one."

"Who was that lady, the one who left us in the cold?"

"She is a hunter, banphrionsa beag. Just one of many that your máthair, athair, and kin are fighting to destroy." The Guardian's tone took on a sharp tone as she added, "All of you were stolen in the night by that soith olc. She sought to exploit you, use you as bait to defeat your parents, but we, the Guardians of the Realm, were too close. In the end, Eve and her horrible father and brother were forced to leave you, scurrying into the darkness like rats off a sinking ship."

Sadie had never heard the Guardian use such language. The fury in the Elder Caretaker's voice fueled the young dragoness' own rage. Picking up the knife the cook used to clean vegetables, Sadie stood by the fire, staring at the blade, imagining the blood of her enemies dripping from the cold steel, creating a morose mosaic across the ice and snow.

"I can see your thoughts, little princess. Feel your need to fight, to defend what you love, but your battle is not today."

"But when?" Sadie pleaded. "Why can I not fight for those I love?"

Sitting down in her huge, oak rocking chair, the Guardian patted her lap and after the young dragoness was comfortably seated, began to slowly rock back and forth. "Because mo ghrá, it is not your time. You still have much to learn and need time to grow. Your Destiny has been written in the stars. Fate and the Universe have grand plans for you."

Pushing her long pewter braids off her shoulder, Sadie looked up at the Guardian and asked, "But am I not needed now? Can I not help Máthair and Athair?" Looking at the other females sleeping quietly in their little beds, she continued, "Can I not help their families? I may be small but I am powerful. Athair said I was born as ferocious as a lioness and as cunning as the eagle. I am Dragon."

Smiling sweetly, the Guardian took the kitchen knife from where her little fingers still clung to the wooden handle and placed it back on the table. "Yes, banphrionsa beag, you have more strength in your little finger than most warriors possess in their entire bodies, but you have just seen your fifth year and there are things you need to know. Things your parents need to teach you so that not only will you be a great warrior but also a great leader."

Ladies of the Sky

She'd heard it all before. Promises that her parents would be back, that she would be trained to fight, that life would go back to what she had known before the attacks. But Sadie knew something was wrong. The war had gone on for too long. The letters from her parents and the other girls' mothers and fathers had stopped coming. It was time Sadie learned to be the leader she had been born to be. Time for her to take control of her future. The Guardian may think of her as a little girl, but the Elder Caretaker could not be more wrong.

Named Scathach Sorcha Ashford after her father and his father before him, the little princess was soon called Sadie because of her spunk and insatiable curiosity. Never far from her parents and always among the people of their clan, she had known nearly from birth that she would one day lead the Ashford Dragons. Her athair was loved among his people, revered as a fair, just, and loving Head Elder, and Sadie wanted nothing more than to follow in his footsteps in every way.

She longed to look into his ruddy features and deep blue eyes, to hear the soft, beautiful song her máthair sang as she gently rocked her daughter to sleep. Sadie needed to know…

"Hello, Earth to Sadie. Are you listening to me?"

Phryne's voice abruptly pulled the dragoness from her memories and had her taking a deep breath as her sister went on without waiting for an answer. "That old wooden door and rusted lock aren't going to hold him for long. His dragon is healing both itself and the man at an amazing rate." Phryne poked at the fire again. "Have you thought about what you're going to do when he breaks free?"

"It won't come to that."

"Because…" Phryne let her unasked question hang in the air, giving Sadie a wide-eyed look and a shrug.

Standing and shaking her head, the dragoness sighed. "Because I'm going to use another tranquilizer dart. We are going to carry him to the lair of the Blue Thunder Dragons, place his unconscious body outside their clinic, and leave."

"First of all, you've been tranquilizing him? I know how strongly you feel about staying away from the dragons. I get it. You don't want to lead a clan or Heavens forbid, the whole damn species, but don't you think he can scent you? Can find his way back whenever he wants?"

"No."

"No? That's all I get?"

Looking at the fire, she remembered the male's long eye lashes as they curled on his high cheekbones, the feel of his rough skin under her fingertips, and the electricity that had skittered up her arm, making her imagine laying her lips to his. It was all so disconcerting, so foreign...*so frightening*. Speaking without looking at Phryne, she said, "I have also used my magic to mask my scent, just as I will do for both of us when we deliver him to his clan." She speared the Pegasus shifter with a look that she hoped would end their conversation and added, "Now, get ready so we can return him to his own and get back to *our* lives."

Getting up, she'd made it exactly three steps toward the cave when Phryne asked, "Are you sure that's what you want to do?"

Ignoring her sister's question, the dragoness called forth her magic, making herself undetectable, then entered the cavern. Once outside the cave where their supplies were stored, she used her preternatural speed to throw open the door, blow the dart at his neck, and slam the door shut before the male knew what was happening.

Counting to ten, Sadie let out the breath she'd been holding when she heard the telltale sound of his body crashing to the stone floor. Opening the door once again, she stood staring. Her dragon pushed against the confines of her mind, reaching for the man and his dragon, grumbling low in her throat and swishing her mighty tail.

"No, we are not keeping him. A man is the last thing we want or need."

Blowing smoke, the iridescent multi-colored dragon lowered her head and growled, pounding the spaded tip of her tail in anger. Dragging the talons of her left front paw as if she wanted to charge against the confines of Sadie's mind, the dragon's low, barely understandable snarl echoed through the dragoness' consciousness, *"Mianach."*

"He is not yours."

"Are you so sure about that, *sianach deirfiúr?*"

"Shut up, Phryne, and grab his feet. We are putting an end to this madness once and for all."

"As you wish," her sister snickered.

If only it were that simple...

Chapter Two

"Orion…Orion, wake up. Damn you, wake up!"

The voice sounded far away but also very adamant that he needed to open his eyes. Floating to the surface, pushing away the last vestiges of sleep, the ancient Guardsman tried to distinguish between his dreams…his nightmares…and his new reality. The feel of a soft cloth upon his brow, strong hands gripping his shoulder, and his dragon pouring white healing magic into his system—forcing the herbs from his veins, allowing him to finally breakthrough the tranquilizer and slowly open his eyes—all assaulted his senses in unison.

His eyes opened and gradually, after blinking several times, his vision cleared. Closing his eyes and counting to three, sure he was seeing a vision, the dragon cracked open one lid and whispered in awe, "Drago? Is…is that you?"

Nodding and smiling with his dark eyes shining, the man Orion had called friend, brother, and Commander for the better part of his life, answered, his voice shaking with emotion. "Yes, it is."

Helping him sit up, the Guardsman Orion had known as the Assassin, clapped him on the back and continued, "I thought you were lost, but then I should have known. Not only could nothing get the best of you but that you were also planning a grand entrance."

Looking around, taking in the white walls and light gray counters, inhaling the scent of disinfectants and medicines and watching others he immediately recognized as dragons and shifters, Orion asked, "Where am I?" Clearing his throat, he added, "How did I get here?"

His Commander furrowed his brows as he asked, "You do not know?" Then over Orion's shoulder inquired, "Are you sure there has been no trauma to his head? Anything that would affect his memory?"

Looking over his shoulder, Orion saw a tall, curvy witch with long strawberry curls and bright green eyes whose scent smelled not only of night blooming jasmine and sage, but also another dragon, one he'd known very well many years ago. Seeing the mating mark on her neck, Orion blurted out, "You are Doxie's mate? The old bastard is still alive and has been given the gift of one so lovely as you?"

"Alive and kicking, you sorry son of a lizard," came a grumbling reply as the tall bearded man with wild hair named Maddox but called the mad dragon because of his permanent state of irritation, wrapped his arms around Orion. Hugging him

27

tightly, his old friend mumbled, "Glad to see you, brother." Then wrapping his arm around his mate as she walked up beside him, the mad dragon smiled one of the few real smiles Orion had ever seen grace his face and added, "This is Calysta, my mate. Callie, this is Orion, or the Shadow, as we all called him."

Smiling despite his confusion, Orion chuckled. "It has been almost a century since anyone called me that," at the use of his old nickname then taking Maddox's mate's outstretched hand he said, "but it is a true pleasure to meet the woman who tamed the mad dragon."

Laughing out loud as her mate grumbled, the witch said, "I'm not sure I tamed him, but I do love him an awful lot."

"As he loves you even more, from the look of things," the Shadow replied, trying hard to take it all in while looking for the woman who had shot him, then helped him, then held him captive, and then apparently returned him to his people.

And I am the one they call the Shadow…

Appropriately tagged with the moniker because of his ability to completely disappear from sight in either of his forms, Orion had just regained his special power when his mystery dragoness shot him in the bum. He had been without his inherited ability during his decades of torture at the hands of the monks. These religious zealots who believed they were ridding the world of evil by torturing and killing supernatural beings had been thorough, to say the least, reducing him to little more than a human with their black magic. After being handed off to them over a century ago by the wizards who attacked and captured him and his brethren, the monks kept the Shadow doused in herbs, surrounded by sigils, and imprisoned in a silver-lined dungeon to suppress his and his dragon's magic.

He could still feel the fire of the liquid silver being poured into the wounds they had carved into his back over and over again. There was no doubt in his mind the marks remained on his flesh, but he knew his dragon had removed all taint of evil from his blood. Refusing to be sucked into a black hole of nightmares and torture, Orion shoved it all aside and again asked, "Where am I?"

"You are at the lair of the Blue Thunder Dragons. Ronan's oldest son, Rian, is now the Head Elder and leader." Drago gave him a wary look before asking, "That was where you were heading, yes?" When Orion took a second too long to answer, the Assassin added, "What is the last thing you remember?"

"I was shot by an arrow and passed out then awoke in a cavern that served as some type of storage. My wounds, both new and old, had been bandaged and there was food. I scented a female," he rushed on, not wanting them to know how much he wanted, no…*needed*, to know who she was, to finally see her face, to *know* if what he felt for her was real or simply something manifesting from the trauma he had endured. "But I never saw her. For the next three days, as I recovered and my wound healed, I slept an overly abundant amount of time and every time I did awake, it was to find the same lingering scent, my bandages changed, and something fresh to eat and drink."

"She shot you, but you never saw her?" Drago asked, working hard not to smile. "You have always been the one of us least likely to find yourself in the enemy's sights and not only did someone get the jump on you, but *she* also took care of you without *you* seeing her?"

"Yes." The Shadow worked hard to keep the irritation he felt out of his voice. It was like the last century had not occurred. He was back with his Commander, Doxie was there, and as usual, they were teasing him about something.

Frustration was soon replaced with memories. This time, he thought of his savior's sweet scent and the recognition that she was also dragon before adding, "I was standing against a tree, cloaked and waiting for her to take a shot." With the memory replaying in his mind, Orion's mood began to lighten. "The deer she was aiming at moved a half step and the next thing I knew, I felt the sting of her arrow." He stopped, bracing for what was to come next, sure his brethren would have more fun at his expense. Instead, the Assassin seemed perplexed.

"And before that?" Drago pressed.

Clearing his throat before answering, Orion explained, "I spent a century at the hands of a radical sect of Roman monks who inhabit a derelict castle at least two hundred miles from where I was shot." He looked at his friends, his brethren, those he thought he might never see again, and went on, "I escaped from the catacombs nearly six weeks ago and made my way west on foot. It took much longer than I expected because of how drained both myself and my dragon were."

Then thinking of all his other brethren, the Enforcers, dragon kin's elite fighting Force, he asked, "And what of the others? Are we all that have been spared? Or escaped?"

"No..." Drago's words were overshadowed by the bellow of a voice Orion had never thought to hear again.

"They said you were alive and I called them liars." Kayne laughed out loud as he sauntered into the clinic with his usual cocky grin and mischief in his eyes. Holding out his hand and pulling the Shadow off the table and into a hug the instant Orion's hand touched the demi-god's, Kayne slapped him on the back then held him at arm's length and teased, "Nice beard, guy. And that hair is a sight. We really need to get you a razor and a shower."

Laughing despite the overload of information and emotion he was experiencing, Orion joked, "At least I can tell everyone I was locked in a dungeon." He winked. "What's your excuse?"

The entire group erupted in laughter as Kayne, the son of Lugh, the Celtic God of the Sun, gave Orion another hug before stepping back. Looking to Drago as the levity died down, the Shadow couldn't help but ask hopefully, "Any other brothers going to come waltzing in?"

"Not today, but I have it on good authority that Angus and his she-wolf, Kyran and his banshee, as well as Quinn and his little elf, will be here within the week. When we found you, I put out the call and have since heard from them all."

"They have found their mates?" Drago nodded as Orion went on, "And you, also." It wasn't a question, because the Shadow could feel the happiness that only the other half of one's soul can bring living within his Commander.

"Yes, I have found my Alicia. You will be meeting her soon." Drago's smile dimmed and there was a hint of sadness as he added, "Unfortunately, I have no news of Uther or Atticus yet, but I remain hopeful. I have to believe one or all of us would know if they had gone onto the Heavens."

Patting the Commander on the shoulder, Orion readily agreed. "The belief that at least some of you still remained on this earth is what kept me going for all those years. I am sure it is the same for them. We will all be a united Force once again, of that you can be sure."

Calysta appeared before him and after sticking a thermometer in his mouth, turned to his brethren with a hand on her hip and ordered, "You all need to at least wait out in the hall. Niall is going to be back at nightfall and if I haven't given Orion a complete check-up by then, there will be hell to pay."

"You heard the lady. Out, you mangy dragons," Maddox ordered with a growl before stopping to kiss his witch goodbye then looking at Orion and grinning. "You listen to my mate and she'll fix you right up." Patting him on the knee, the mad dragon spun on his heel and exited the room, shutting the door on his way out.

Waiting until Calysta removed the thermometer and he heard his brethren exit the clinic, Orion asked, "Is the woman who dropped me off still here?"

Shaking her head, the witch stopped and looked up from the clipboard she was writing on before answering, "There was no woman. I found you laying on the picnic table behind the building, wrapped in a hand-woven woolen blanket, completely unconscious and quite alone."

"This morning?"

"Oh no," Calysta quickly responded with his wrist between her thumb and two middle fingers as she took his pulse. "I found you night before last. You have been here for almost forty-eight hours."

"Do you still have the blanket?"

Looking perplexed, the witch recorded his pulse and answered with furrowed brows, "Well, yes, but if you're looking for a scent or a clue, you won't find it. Both Drago and Maddox have thoroughly examined it and neither can find any evidence of anyone but you ever touching it."

"May I try?" Orion was working hard not to yell and scream that he needed to see that blanket, needed to touch it, scent it right that very minute or he might spontaneously combust. He wanted Calysta to understand that it was his only link to the woman he so desperately needed to find…needed to see with his own eyes, that he would do just about anything to get his hands on it.

Thankfully, Maddox's mate didn't need convincing as she nodded, turned, and while heading out the door, called over her shoulder, "Be right back."

True to her word, Calysta was back in less than two minutes carrying a large plastic bag containing the same woolen blanket Orion had found himself covered with after being shot. Removing the cover from the sack, the Shadow was nearly intoxicated by the scent of effervescent apple blossoms, female dragon, and heaven that left him wondering how no one else had smelled it.

Looking up, he caught Calysta smiling at him with a knowing look as she nodded, "They couldn't scent anything but you sure can, can't you?"

Having never been very good with subterfuge, Orion simply nodded. "Yes, I can." He watched her smile widen and then asked, "Can we keep this between us for just a little while? I need to figure out what I am going to do about it."

"Sure, I can use Healer – patient confidentiality, even with Maddox." She stepped closer and leveled her gaze at him. "But if you go off half-cocked or do something stupid then all bets are off. I'll sell you out faster than the last tube of Mac's Lady Danger Red lipstick on Black Friday."

"Excuse me, but what is Black Friday? Who is Mac? And I promise I do not wish to wear your lipstick." Orion was sure there was a code in her speech that he was supposed to understand but feared he was more lost than ever. Then Calysta laughed out loud and he could only sit and wait as she dried the tears from her face and took a deep breath.

Patting his knee, she chuckled. "I am so sorry, Orion. I forget you've been out of circulation for a century or so. I didn't mean to confuse you. Let me just say, I am glad to know you don't want to wear my lipstick. You will find out soon enough what Black Friday is and as for who is Mac? It's a makeup company and therefore, another something you will never be bothered with." She looked more closely at the scars covering his arms and legs while adding, "What I should've said was I'll keep your secrets as long as you take care of yourself. If you don't, then I have to tell Maddox and you know as well as I do that it never ends well when he gets involved."

He could see why the Universe had paired this beautiful, intelligent, and witty witch with his longtime friend. She was the one person in the world who knew all of Doxie's faults and saw the real, true man underneath. Nodding, Orion smiled. "I will strive to keep our bargain."

"Good." Calysta walked around the table and began touching the marks on his back with her plastic glove covered fingers.

Sitting as still as possible, Orion held his breath until the witch asked, "Have you seen these glyphs for yourself?"

"No," he shoved aside the dark memories threatening to rise at the reminder and hurried on, "I only felt them as the monks were carving them into my flesh and then adding the silver."

"I am so sorry."

Her touch was gentle and he could feel her pouring her own special brand of white healing magic into them, which prompted him to add, "They repeated the process five times before they were satisfied that I would be marked forever."

He heard her footsteps and the sound of her removing her gloves a few seconds before she appeared back in front of him. Looking him right in the eye, Calysta explained, "They are runes of magic and healing suppression. Because there are so many that mean the same thing, I believe they were trying to render both you and your dragon completely helpless with the hope that one or both of you would expel your magic so that they could steal it." She made more notes on her clipboard. "I am going to check some of the ancient texts I have at the house and the coven to be sure, but for now, I feel no magic but your own and that of your dragon. You are very strong beings. Thankfully, the monks' attempts failed."

Breathing a sigh of relief as Calysta confirmed what he already knew, Orion held out his hand and as her fingers closed around his, said, "Thank you very much. I truly appreciate all you have done for me."

"It was my pleasure." Putting her pen in her pocket and holding the clipboard close to her chest, she added, "Try to get some rest. The girls will be in with your dinner soon and then my sister Della, who will be your night nurse, will be in with your last dose of healing herbs." She patted the bed next to his hand and continued, "I have no doubts as soon as Niall sees you in the morning, you'll be out of here and into a more comfortable bed either at our house or at Drago and Alicia's."

"That sounds wonderful." Orion put his legs on the bed and laid back. "I look forward to seeing Niall again. It had been years since I'd seen him before I was taken. I always enjoyed our philosophical conversations."

"He is good for that," Calysta snickered before stopping with her hand on the doorknob and half-turning back toward him. "If you need anything, please don't hesitate to have Della call us or," she tapped her temple, "just call Maddox."

"My mind speak has still not recovered." He saw her start to apologize and hurried to add, "Please do not be sorry. You did not know, and I can already feel the old pathways coming back together. I am sure it will return any day now."

"I'm still sorry. It was short-sided of me to not have asked that during your examination." She looked at him. "And I am sure you're right. You're healing at a fantastic rate so it's only time before you're as good as new."

"Thank you again," he reassured. "Now, go to your mate. If I know Doxie, he is pacing and looking at the clock."

Laughing as she exited the room, Calysta agreed, "You know him well."

Listening to the sounds of the witch's footsteps and everyone telling her to have a good night, Orion waited patiently. He ate dinner, met Della, took his medicine, and almost immediately fell asleep where his dreams revolved around the scent of apples and the need to find the elusive woman who haunted his every thought.

They rushed at him like some sort of disjointed movie, bouncing from one memory to another in vivid, living color. He watched the morning in the woods as an observer just before feeling the sting of the arrow. The cave where he'd been kept flashed before him and he saw himself wake up, surprised to be clean and comfortable, overjoyed to have food at the ready and thanking the Heavens that he was at least semi-free for the first time in more than a century.

Waiting patiently, Orion hoped beyond hope that his subconscious had caught sight of the woman, the dragoness….his obsession, but, alas, it had not. Instead, the scene began to fade; it felt as if he was floating and then in the blink of an eye, he saw a grey dragon, *his* beast, flying high in the sky joined by a female whose scales glittered in the sunlight with every color of the rainbow, looking like a kaleidoscope of happiness, joy and…hope.

Waking with a start, the Shadow jumped from his bed, slipped his feet into the boots and clothes he knew from their scent that Drago had left for him, and made his way out the back door of the clinic.

Holding the blanket the dragoness had wrapped him in close to his heart, inhaling her intoxicating scent and stealing away into the night, the Shadow whispered, "I will find you, *mo Dragoness*, of that you can be sure."

Chapter Three

"Are you going to stop moping any time soon?"

"I am not moping, I'm looking for game," Sadie growled, still irritated that Phryne had tagged along on her hunt. All the dragoness wanted was to be alone and sulk. It was *all* she had wished for since the night they'd returned the male to his kin.

"Okay, whatever you say, but I know moping when I see it," the winged-horse shifter clicked her tongue. "And that," she pointed at Sadie, "is moping at its finest."

"Be. Quiet," Sadie whispered through gritted teeth, eyeing a buck a hundred yards away as she thought of their dwindling food stores after feeding a half-starved male dragon shifter for the better part of four days. She had no regrets for helping him but had to replace what he had eaten as quickly as possible.

Taking a deep breath and holding it, the dragoness pulled her bow string tight and stared at the tuft of fur just above the buck's shoulder. She would only shoot if she was sure to drop the animal where it stood. Making it suffer was out of the question. Apex predator or not, Sadie Ashford, both woman and dragon, had a heart.

Ladies of the Sky

Pulling her gloved hand back a fraction of a millimeter and
letting out the breath she'd been holding in precise timing with
the release of the bow string, Sadie watched her arrow cut a
straight, sharp path through the forest, careening toward her prey.
All it took was a single flash of sunlight deflected from only the
Heavens knew where and the buck was off and running, and
Sadie's arrow was stuck in a tree, leaving the dragoness to curse
like a sailor.

"Dammit all to Hades. Of all the stupid, asinine...If I get my
hands on the son of a bitch who...Bastard. Dumb bastard..."

"Nice language, sis," Phryne snickered.

Ignoring the Pegasus' comment, Sadie stomped across the
fallen leaves and decaying brush, the crunch under the heel of her
boots calming her ire and allowing her to think. Sending out her
preternatural senses to see who or what had caused the
disturbance that scared off her prey, the dragoness promised
retribution.

Pulling her arrow from the hard wood of the Alder tree, Sadie
prayed to the Guardians of the Earth for quick healing and
apologized for the scar she'd left on its majestic trunk. Listening
to the sounds of a waking wilderness, the dew drying from the
leaves, the birds chirping in the trees, the squirrels chittering to
their young, and even a fox yipping to her kits, the dragoness

42

searched as far and wide as she could, but found no clue of who or what had spooked the huge buck.

With the sun rising over the mountain ridge and no game to clean, she quickly revised her plans and called to Phryne, "I am going to check the traps, do some fishing, and then hunt right after nightfall. See you in the morning."

Heading off into a denser part of the forest, she heard the winged-horse shifter scoff, "Annnnndddd, I've been dismissed. Once again with no goodbye, thank you for hanging with me, or kiss my big toe." Phryne's voice got a bit louder as she added, "And I know darned good and well you can hear me, so listen up. I'm only going to put up with your crap for another couple of centuries or so. You hear me. You'll miss me when I'm gone."

Sadie bit her bottom lip to keep from laughing. She knew her sister was right. She would miss Phryne, as she would miss all her sisters were they ever to part ways. "And, I fear that time is coming," she mumbled to herself. "The winds of change are blowing. Fate and Destiny are knocking at the door and I'm afraid they have come with an ultimatum, not a request."

Shaking her head and letting out the breath she'd been holding, Sadie thought about a bit of target practice. Although she preferred her bow for hunting, there was just something about the feel of the cool metal in her hand, the sound of the gun firing, the scent of sulfur, coal, and salt peter in the air, and the power she felt watching the rotting fruits and vegetables explode that calmed her nerves. It was almost as cathartic as a good sword fight, which she had actually entertained. Gwendolyn was an excellent swordswoman, but in Sadie's present mindset, she doubted her ability to simply train.

Even though she had denied Phryne's accusations that she was moping, the dragoness had to admit, at least to herself, that she *was* being cranky, irritable, and yes, mopey, and had been since leaving *him* with the Blue Dragons. It wasn't that she didn't stand by her decision; she truly believed it was the best thing not only for her clan, but also for herself. It was that she missed him and it simply made no sense at all.

Long ago, after the news of her parents' deaths and that of the other girls' families, Sadie made a vow to lead their clan, to give the other six girls a family, to redefine what they all thought of as kin from blood-relatives to those of their hearts. Together, all seven had come together under the light of the full moon, taken a blood oath, and pledged their loyalty not to the Universe and the Heavens, for those they would always hold dear, but to one another.

Seven women with incredible powers, many the last of their kind, all with the ability to shift form and take flight, became much more than refugees or orphans, they became family...sisters-of-the-heart. As the years passed and the Guardian aged, Sadie knew the time was approaching for her to truly take the lead.

And that is how it had been for nearly fifty years. With the dragoness at the helm, the Ladies of the Sky had operated as a clan, lived together, worked together, and grew together, but now, it seemed as if the tide was turning and great changes were on the horizon. Changes Sadie not only did not want, but on some deep, almost inherent level, feared. It made no sense. She had never feared anything, or if she did, had always found a way to fight, conquer, or destroy the obstacle. In this case, none of those options would work, nor did she want to try them. No, this man, this *dragon,* who had invaded their forest and overstayed his welcome, made the princess think of things she had locked away or denounced years ago.

Checking the last of the traps and finding them empty, Sadie made her way to the lake, climbed into her canoe, and paddled across the crystal-clear water. Listening to the stream coursing against the rocks, letting it carry away her worries, she picked a spot under the long drooping limbs of a weeping willow tree to anchor and fish. Baiting the hooks on four different rods, she leaned the poles against the side of her boat, sat back, ate her lunch, and waited.

The longer time passed without a bite, the farther into her thoughts and memories the dragoness fell, until she was once again a teenager, sitting across from the Guardian, having a healthy debate about fated mates and their uselessness...

"But I don't see why I have to swoon over a man, any man for that matter, just because Fate or the Universe, the Heavens or Destiny, have decided he is the one for me. Do I not have a say in the matter? Does it not matter what I think or what I feel?"

Answering as patiently as she answered all questions, the Guardian nodde., "But of course, you have a say in the matter and yes, all the Deities care what you think and feel. That is precisely the point. They have designed not only you, but the perfect mate for you. For who could know you better than the loving hands that molded your beautiful heart and fearsome mind? They have taken all your wants and desires, needs and dreams, everything that makes you the very special being that you are into consideration and then fashioned your perfect complement. The one person who understands you better than even you understand yourself."

Jumping to her feet and throwing her hands in the air, the dragoness railed, "But how could they know that what I want now is what I will want in fifty years, a hundred years, five centuries? What if I hate him? What if he hates me? How would we be of any benefit to one another, dragon kin, or the Universe?"

Smiling as serenely as if they were taking a walk and picking flowers, the Guardian explained, "It is impossible for you to hate him or for him to hate you, my little princess. You were designed for one another. Your ancestors thought the concept of mates was so important that even the Holy Book of Dragon Kin explains this very special gift. The writings explain, 'When the two halves of the same whole meet, there will be instant recognition. Their souls will merge, and only then will the man and dragon know complete peace. They will have found their true home. It will be as if the time before they met their one true mate, the light of their soul, ceases to exist. The life they spent alone no longer is of any consequence. All that will matter from that moment forward will be that they become one in body, mind, and soul in the ways of the Ancients with the One the Universe made for them.'"

"It even goes on to say that each female is not only the light to her mate's soul, but his strength and his guiding force." She stood and stepped into Sadie's path, making the little dragoness stop mid-step and listen. "Do you not see how vitally important you and all your sisters are to the continuation of your races?

47

Not simply to have children as you so crassly put it a few minutes ago, but because you are the life's blood of your people. You, as women, as leaders, as warriors, are stronger when united with the other half of your soul than on your own. When two hearts become one, it is a promise one to another, and neither time, nor space, nor even death can break, for it will last a lifetime. Ever strong, ever resilient, everlasting."

The Guardian placed the side of her index finger under Sadie's chin, lifting her head until the dragoness could see the wisdom shining bright in the depths of the teacher's eyes and added, "You, Princess Scathach Sorcha Ashford, Royal and Rightful Leader of the Mighty Ashford Dragons, will only be given a mate who is filled with joy at your very existence and welcoming of your quick mind, strong will, and fearlessness. He will stand by your side, not in front of you and most definitely not behind you, but at your side, an equal and willing partner in all things."

Moving her hand to cup Sadie's cheek, the Guardian went on, "And, my darling little princess, he will love you infinitely more than the sum of all the raindrops that fall from the Heavens for all your lifetimes together, for you will be his light, his love, and his salvation."

Watching the clouds skate across the sky, Sadie couldn't help but think of the man she and Phryne had returned to his people. It was hard to admit, even to herself, that in the three days since leaving him atop that table, she had thought of little else. Whether waking or sleeping, he was first and foremost in her mind. She found herself sitting in the food storage cavern, unsure of when she'd left the lake, holding the pillow he had used, inhaling his scent, and remembering every nuance of his handsome face while wondering who had been so evil as to inflict such torture upon him that the scars remained despite his powerful magic.

Had she made a mistake? Should she have let him stay? Was he important to her future? Never before had she doubted a decision, but this *one man* was making her question not only her choice, but almost everything she had ever believed.

Should she have revealed herself to him? Talked to him? Made sure he was as good a man as she believed him to be? Question upon question beat at the dragoness until she feared she would lose her mind.

Leaving the cave, she walked to the ridge, pulled the opal pendant of her father now hanging on a chain around her neck from under the soft leather of her vest, and looked at the matching ring her mother had worn every day while bringing up the last image she remembered of them, the one from the picture she kept hidden in her Book of Prayers. She thought of their smiling faces and the look of love they shared with her and between themselves. Her arms tingled, thinking of how her father's calloused fingertips felt on her skin in comparison to her mother's soft touch.

Focusing as hard as she could, Sadie recalled the low timbre of her father's voice and the way his laugh boomed off every wall in the Great Hall, making everyone laugh along. The contralto of her mother's soft tone resonated through both woman and dragon as Sadie whispered the prayer she and Sasha had repeated every night before bed. "Now I lay me down to sleep, I pray the Heavens my soul to keep. Guide me and my dragon through the starry night and wake me when the sun shines bright. Keep all my kin and their kin too, safe and sound and near to you. I thank you for this day, in your loving grace I pray."

For the first time in nearly fifty years, a single tear tumbled down Sadie's cheek as she raised her eyes to the Heavens and pleaded, "Mathair, Athair, if ever I needed you, it is now."

Chapter Four

"And this is what happens when you run off half-cocked," Orion murmured to himself as he followed the scent of the woman who dominated his every thought, action, and dream. "You were even warned," he scoffed.

It wasn't that her scent was hard to follow; it not only filled the senses of both man and dragon, but also their souls. It was that the Guardsman was beginning to wonder if he should have been more prepared before meeting the dragoness he was sure had been made especially for him. He had never been the suave or smooth one of their group; that was Kayne's job. Orion was more the strong, silent type who stood to the back and kept watch. Being the son of the Spiritual Elder of their clan, he had been taught patience and that there would only ever be one woman who captured the heart of both man and beast.

Sure, there had been dalliances over the years. The Heavens knew he had been a typical randy young man during his transformation years, but that had ended almost as quickly as it began when he was initiated into the Guard. It wasn't long before he and the lads were off fighting one battle after another with barely a day between, lasting nearly a century before they were abducted.

Now, he was almost two hundred and fifty years old, traipsing through the woods, unsure what to say when he finally met the person who would complete him in every way possible. Stopping midstride as the sound of a branch snapping under the heel of a boot reached his ears, the Shadow took cover behind a pile of rotten logs and overgrown foliage.

Scenting the air, he found a Pegasus shifter and a Thunderbird, both of which he thought had been extinct for many years. Even more interesting was the fact that they were both female and carried the scent of the woman for whom he searched. Listening to them talk, he recognized their familiarity as being something like the relationship he shared with his brethren and smiled.

"I know she's sitting up on that ridge, meditating and kicking herself over every decision she's made over the last week." Looking through the brambles, he saw it was the woman with short dark hair, the Pegasus, who had spoken.

The Thunderbird, a redhead with braids down to her hips, freckles covering her cheeks and nose, and bright green eyes that glowed as she spoke, chuckled. "Or she's standing in the lake with a spear, taking her anger out on the fish."

"Either way, our Sadie is tied in knots and I wish I knew how to help." The brunette's tone was part worry, part irritation.

"I just wish you could tell me what was going on," the redhead shook her head. "I guess I should be used to it. I'm the last to know everything. Always have been." She snorted. "Which in some cases, with you lot, is a good thing."

"You know what's even better?" The winged-horse shifter stopped as she spoke and from one breath to the next, pulled out her short blade, hurtled it through the air, and yelled, "Don't move, dragon, or I swear the next one will be between your eyes," as her blade stuck firmly into the piece of petrified wood standing less than two scant inches from his head.

Slowly standing, Orion held up one hand while holding the blanket to his chest and carefully explained, "I mean no harm. I simply came to return your blanket and thank you for helping me when I was injured."

Glaring and unmoving, the brunette had a second blade aimed at his head and the Thunderbird's bow had an arrow cocked and pointing at his heart. Deciding all he could do was stand absolutely still and plead his case, Orion took a deep breath, cleared his throat, and asked, "You are the ones who saved me when I'd been shot and returned me to my people, yes?"

The redhead barked, "No," at the precise the moment the Pegasus nodded, "Yes," while trying to hide a grin.

The Thunderbird's head snapped to the side and he immediately heard the telltale buzz of mind speak. From the expression on the brunette's face, he knew she was on the receiving end of what his mother used to call a tongue-lashing but was taking it all in stride and still holding back her smile.

In less than a minute, they were both staring at him again, neither one looking anymore pleased to see him than they had before. The Pegasus demanded, "What are you doing here? We returned you to your people. Don't you know how to stay put?"

It took everything in Orion not to laugh out loud at the brunette's bold attitude. He liked her. She was quick on the draw, good with a blade, and not afraid to speak her mind. He thought about telling her so, but somehow figured she would not appreciate his assessment. Instead, he said, "I apologize for trespassing. I simply wanted to thank those responsible for my speedy recovery and return this." He again used the blanket as the excuse for his intrusion while telling as much of the truth as he could.

"You're welcome," the brunette snapped. "Drop the blanket and head back to your people."

Taking a deep breath as he stepped out from behind the brambles, the Guardsman feared he might have to confess his true intentions, but the sound of huge wings flapping overhead followed by a screech that nearly shook the forest floor drew everyone's attention right before a huge Strix, an ancient owl shifter with incredible powers, landed between he and the female shifters. Magic filled the air as the miraculous bird disappeared and in its place appeared a tall, platinum blonde with grey eyes and skin the color of caramel.

Her gaze shot from the others to him, turning dark and stormy. The clouds overhead covered the rising sun and the air turned cool as she held up her hand and asked, "Who are you and why are you here?"

"He is here to thank us for helping him," the redhead laughed sarcastically. "Did you know we had helped any men lately, Pearl?"

Moving only her lips, the Strix he now knew as Pearl, slowly shook her head and grumbled, "I did not, Gwendolyn, but I am guessing that our lovely sister, Phryne, did." She narrowed her gaze even more, still pointing at Orion and asked, "Tell me, Phryne, does he look familiar?"

Dropping her arm and thus her knife, the Pegasus named Phryne rolled her eyes and sighed. "Okay, I knew, but *she* made me swear. Didn't want to involve the rest of you." She put her hands on her hips. "We kept him locked in the storage cave and returned him to his people as soon as he was well enough to travel."

Pearl slowly turned her head to look at the women she'd called sister, reminding him of the owl she'd just been, and asked, "You did not think he would just come back? He's a dragon after all." She looked back at him and curled her nose before adding, "A *male* dragon." Scoffing, she looked back to her sister and said, "The only dragon I've ever trusted is Sadie. The rest, especially the men, are nosey and domineering and…"

Sadie…now, I know her name…

Holding up her hands, Phryne interrupted, "We sedated him, hid our scent, covered our trail, and dropped him off without anyone seeing us." She scowled at Orion, "He should *not* have been able to find his way back here."

"Yet, here he is," Gwendolyn snipped, her Scottish brogue thicker than before as she still held her bow at the ready.

Letting her hands fall to her sides, Pearl relaxed her stance and walked to stand beside the Thunderbird, placing her hand on Gwendolyn's bow and forcing it down, much to her sister's chagrin. Shaking her head, the Strix said, her British accent more defined and her tone almost lilting, "It would not have mattered if you beat him over the head and doused yourself in kerosene." Her eyes shot to his, "This Guardsman is on the hunt."

"He is what and what?" Phryne turned to Pearl. "Are you saying he seriously is one the Enforcers?"

Orion eyes snapped to hers and before he'd had time to think, was demanding, "You know of the Enforcers?" He took a threatening step forward. "Who are you? How do you know of us?"

It was when Pearl raised a crossbow he hadn't seen until that moment, Phryne pulled her blade back out of its sheath, and Gwendolyn's bow was back at the ready, that the Shadow realized he had nothing but a blanket. Holding up his hand, Orion quickly apologized, "I'm sorry. Excuse the offense. It's just that, well," he took a breath, praying for the words that would ease the tension darting between he and the female shifters then began again, "Yes, to answer your question, I am one of the Enforcers. My name is Orion and again, I truly did not mean to impose by coming here. All I wanted to do was thank you for helping me."

He dropped his hand and took a step back. "When you found me…well, let's just say I had been running for my life. I was looking for my kin after having been imprisoned for almost a century."

57

"So, the stories of your death and that of your brothers was wrong?" Pearl asked, her curiosity outweighing whatever threat she thought he posed. "The Guardian always told us that she and her people believed you to all still be alive. Their warriors had even searched for you for many years."

Nodding as a feeling of admiration for the women before him grew, Orion continued, "No, we were not killed. Only bewitched, imprisoned, and tortured for nearly a century, at least in my case. I haven't spoken to all my brethren, but it appears we all suffered different fates. However, we survived…for the most part."

He thought about Uther and Atticus and prayed to the Heavens for their safe return as the Strix moved closer and held out her free hand to him. Tingling, like butterflies landing on his arms, signaled that Pearl was using her healing magic to help his wounded soul. When she spoke, it was with reverence. "I am so very sorry for what you have endured, Guardsman, and I understand your mission, but I must tell you, what you seek will not be easily won."

Walking up on either side, their weapons thankfully stowed, the Pegasus and the Thunderbird spoke in unison, something he guessed happened a lot. "What are you talking about, Pearl? What mission?"

Orion felt the weight of the Strix's stare then heard her voice in his mind, *"This is your tale to tell, dragon. The decision is yours, but I suggest you make it quickly."*

Opening his mouth to speak, Orion instead spun on his heels and held his breath as the scent of apple blossoms filled the air. Looking as deep into the forest as his preternatural vision would allow, the Guardsman saw the movement of a dense thicket a second before *she* burst through the overgrown foliage.

Unable to move, he merely stared as the dragoness moved closer, still unaware of his presence. She was a dream come to life; her long pewter hair with silver highlights braided around her face like the female warriors of old and hanging long down her back. Her warm brown eyes were full of life, wisdom, and determination as she walked through the forest as if she owned it, signaling to all who was in charge.

He could feel her strength and resolve that served as the perfect complement to her warm heart and the deep emotions she worked so hard to hide, even with the yards that still separated them. His hands fisted with the need to touch her sun-kissed skin. His body warmed with the need to feel the contrast of her womanly curves against the unyielding muscles of his body. His mouth watered as she licked her perfectly plump peach lips and his dragon roared in recognition of the dragoness he knew dwelled within Sadie's soul.

As if she heard his thoughts, the dragoness' eyes met his. Recognition flared to life. Coming to a complete halt, she stared for what seemed like forever before leveling her gaze and growling, "Did I not make it clear that you were not welcome here?"

Chapter Five

Ignoring the man who had become the bane of her existence, Sadie stalked toward her three sisters and demanded, "What is he doing here?" pointing behind her back as she glared at the ones she held most dear.

"You know exactly what he is doing here, Sadie," Pearl smiled. "And please, do not try to act as if you do not."

Adding Pearl to the list of people she was ignoring, the dragoness turned to Phryne and raised a single eyebrow. Her sister looked at the male then at Pearl then at Gwendolyn and finally back to Sadie before, rambling, "Look, I told you this whole plan of yours was never going to work. As for 'what'," she used the air quotes the dragoness really hated while still talking so fast it was hard to keep up, "he is doing here, I have no idea. As for *who* he is here to see, well, ummm…that is obvious. As for *how* he got here, you will have to talk to him or Pearl because I have no earthly idea and they seem to have all the answers." She took a breath before quickly adding, "And as for me, I already got yelled at by Gwendolyn for keeping secrets and I have a headache, so I am going home."

61

With a, "Humph!" Phryne spun around and strode off, leaving Sadie to look at Gwendolyn, who shook her head and admitted, "She's right. I did yell." The Thunderbird shook her finger at Sadie. "We do not keep secrets. That's rule number one and you," she stopped shaking her finger and pointed with gusto, "kept a whopper from all of us and forced Phryne to go along with you. It is just not right, *deirfiúr*. Just not right."

Repeating her sister's actions, Gwendolyn jogged to catch Phryne as Sadie watched and tried to figure out what she was going to say to Pearl. Unfortunately, as the Strix was apt to do because of all her over the top intuitive powers, Pearl beat the dragoness to the punch and appeared at her side with a knowing look in her eyes and a smile.

"If the Guardian was here, she would tell you that you cannot outrun Fate or Destiny." The Strix reached out and wrapped her long elegant fingers around Sadie's hand, giving her a little squeeze of reassurance before saying, "You know what is the right thing to do. I believe you have since you first laid eyes on him."

Pearl squeezed her hand a second time and closed the scant distance between them. "Sadie Ashford, you are the strongest person I know. It is time you let the world see it, too." Kissing her on the cheek, the Strix whispered, "He is a good man with a good heart. Take a chance. You might just find you like it."

Rolling her eyes even as she felt the truth in Pearl's words, Sadie watched yet another sister walk away, unblinking until the Strix disappeared into the forest. The heat of the male's stare on her back should have irritated the dragoness, should have made her feel uncomfortable, should have at the very least felt foreign. Instead, it was like the first hello, or the first blossom in springtime, or the first sunrise after a thunderstorm…it was a new beginning and it scared the living hell out of her.

Slowly turning toward the male, Sadie looked him right in the eye and, even though she had the best intentions to be kind, her words still sounded like an accusation when she questioned, "How *did* you track us? I have been hiding my scent for over a century and no one, *no one*, has ever been able to follow my trail." She took a step forward. "How did *you* do it?"

Before he could answer, she added, "And *why*? Your lair is over a hundred and fifty miles away? Why would you come back here?" Another step forward. "What could you possibly want from us?" She felt her temper taking over. Tried hard to control it as her dragon pushed the princess a step closer still.

Trying to be patient and wait for his answer, she took a long look at the man who simply refused to leave her alone. Where there had once been a long scraggly beard, there was now a neatly trimmed mustache and goatee perfectly accentuating his strong jawline and a cupid's bow that made his lips extremely hard to look away from. His hair had been trimmed and even though pulled back at the nape of his neck, was still wavy and refusing to be tamed.

Her gaze traveled to his neck where she noticed his wounds were almost healed and his scars not so red and angry. His fingers clenched and unclenched as he held the woolen blanket to his chest that she had left wrapped around him that fateful night. When he spoke, the rumbling timbre of his voice rolled over and around her until Sadie had to take a deep breath and refocus to catch what he was saying.

"I came back, because…well," he chuckled nervously then cleared his throat, his Gaelic brogue more pronounced when he began again. "I couldn't stay away. I had to see who had shot me with her arrow." He finally took a step forward as he snickered, "But was kind enough to take care of me afterward."

Looking up at the sky, taking a deep breath and slowly letting it out, he lowered his gaze and continued, "I tracked you by scent." He held up his hand as Sadie began to argue and shook his head. "I know you are going to tell me that you magically disguised it or hid it some other way and I believe you did." He nodded and took another step in her direction. "None of my brethren could catch your scent, neither on this," he held the blanket out between them, "nor anywhere around where you left me, and we are the Enforcers, the best of the best, so I believe you did what you could to hide from me."

He stopped talking and just stared. Sadie knew he wanted to say more, could feel the words nearly bubbling out of him, but for some reason also knew that he wanted her to ask him how he did it. So, she did. "But you're here? Is that because you are as you say, 'the best of the best'?"

Dropping the hand holding the blanket to his side, the Guardsman shook his head and smiled. His change in expression coupled with the glint in his eye and the dimple in his cheek nearly stole her breath, making it hard to focus when he softly answered, "No, that makes me your mate."

That one word, the one Sadie had been avoiding since her arrow first made contact with his flesh, echoed over and over in her mind. It took hold of her heart and shook her to the very bottom of her soul. It was the truth she had been avoiding, running from and feared more than anything she had ever faced. How could the Universe, or Fate, or Destiny, or whoever was in charge of the craziness that had become her life, possibly think she was ready for a mate?

Needing to think but refusing to appear weak or scared, Sadie nodded, "Is that so, Guardsman?"

"Orion."

"What?" she spat, not understanding his answer, and thinking of punching him in the jaw. He smirked, "My name is Orion, not Guardsman or dragon or whatever *lovely* names you have come up with for me." He had the audacity to wink at her as he added, "And yes, Sadie Ashford, that is so."

He paused and tilted his head to the side. His smile widened and his eyes narrowed as if he was thinking just before he nodded, "And, if I'm not mistaken, this is not new information to you."

Thankfully, the Leader of the Ladies of the Sky had a good poker face, because Orion's words coupled with his confidence and the way his brogue made everything sound mysterious and romantic, was making it hard for Sadie to hold onto her anger. Not to mention, the pushing and pining from her dragon as the beast reached for not only one of its own kind, but the mate of her heart.

Using the strategy that had saved her ass and that of her sisters more than once, Sadie metaphorically wrapped both hands around her anger, leaned forward, and growled, "You know nothing about me, Guardsman." Purposely using his title and not his name, she continued, "And you are trespassing on our land. You are not welcome and you need to leave."

Closing the distance between them, still sporting his smirk, Orion slowly shook his head. "I am not going anywhere until we talk. You can try to get rid of me. Hell, shoot me with another arrow, but I. Am. Not. Leaving."

Refusing to back down, Sadie returned Orion's stare, no longer holding back the rage that was quickly coming to a boil at his insolence but actually pushing it toward him, challenging him, provoking him, throwing down the gauntlet to see what he was truly made of. She watched the pupils of his eyes elongate, felt the power of his dragon answering her challenge, and let the corners of her mouth curl into a predatory smile.

Not wanting to be left out, her dragon poured magic into the princess, snarling and preening her long elegant neck. Sadie's sight became more vivid, her hearing more intense, her sense of smell intensely acute as her focus narrowed on the dragon before her. Anticipation and the thrill of a worthy adversary fueled her hypersensitivity. She noticed the tiny flecks of gold swirling in the eyes of both man and dragon. His ragged breathing echoed in her ears as the scent of the forest at night combined with a campfire burning with sweet, fragrant wood filled her senses.

The muscle in his jaw jumped. He dropped the blanket as his hands opened and closed to the tempo of her pounding heart. Fire danced in his eyes as just the tip of his tongue slipped between his lips, leaving a glistening trail of moisture on his plump bottom lip. Heat flashed between them. Orion's eyes widened and his nostrils flared. Sadie's body warmed and in the blink of an eye, his arms were wrapped around her waist, his hard body pressed against hers and his lips crushing hers in an all-encompassing kiss of fire, passion, and possession.

It no longer became about challenging him but enticing him, teasing him, making him as crazy with desire as she was. He dominated her mouth like he already owned her heart and soul. Desire, previously unknown to her, flared to life, roaring through her like a wildfire, devouring all she'd ever known, making her want more of its heavenly flame.

Her hands tangled in his hair, pulled the silken strands from the leather strap and wound them around her fingers, holding him close as his lips left hers, blazing a trail of need across her jaw and down her neck. His rough, calloused fingers dove under the leather of her vest. Sparks, the electricity of their connection, burst through her body, culminating in a fireball of arousal in the depths of her soul as he moved her backward until she felt the bark of a tree at her back and her arousal wetting the crotch of her panties.

His erection pushed against her center as the dragon rolled his hips. His fingers dug into the tight globes of her ass and lifted her feet from the ground. Immediately wrapping her legs around his waist, matching the tempo of his hips, her fingers grabbed at his shoulders as she mewled, "Yes…yes…Orion…yes…"

The warmth of his breath raised goose bumps all over her body as his lips touched her ear and he growled, "Oh yes...Sadie…you are mine, *mo dragoness, mo banphrionsa, mianach.*"

Something in his tone, his conviction, the way he claimed her as his like no one else ever had, freed something deep inside of Sadie. Her movements became frantic. She ripped his jacket and shirt from his body. Her nails bit into the skin on his shoulders as her lips and teeth kissed and tasted across his shoulders and beautifully muscular chest.

Her fingers reached between their bodies, fighting with the button on his pants, wanting to feel all of him, needing to answer the mating call setting her aflame from the inside out. Orion's hand fisted her hair, pulling her lips back to his, ripping the clothes from her body and letting his jeans slide down his legs.

Tearing his lips from hers, he commanded, "Sadie, look at me." Her eyes snapped to him as he growled, "*Tá tú mianach.*"

Needing his kiss more than to answer, she pushed forward only to have him pull his head even farther back and snarl, "*Tá tú mianach,* Sadie Ashford. Say it."

Testing his resolve, she pushed forward a second time, passion and wanton desire demanding she have this man, but still Orion resisted, this time roaring, "*Tá tú mianach.* You. Are. Mine. SAY IT!"

Unable to resist any longer, her need so strong it threatened her very sanity, Sadie roared in return, "*Tá mé mise,* dammit. I am yours, Orion!"

Crying out in utter bliss as his cock slammed into her, the dragoness felt her body stretch to accommodate his intrusion and her pussy pulse around him, pulling him deeper still, wanting...demanding all he had to give. Holding her gaze captive, Orion pulled back and thrust even faster and with more force than before. Fire roared through her veins as he drove into her faster and faster.

She felt his hands on her back, protecting her skin from the bark of the tree as the slap of skin on skin echoed through the forest. Harder, faster, over and over, they could not get enough of one another. Her body tightened. Her heart beat with a fury she'd never before felt. Her nails slid down his back, feeling the scars, loving all of him. She inhaled the sweet coppery scent of his blood as the rainbow scales of her dragon covered the backs of her hands and flowed up her arms.

Orion's hand slid between their bodies; his fingers slipped through the wet curls covering her mound, slid around her throbbing clit, rubbing tiny circles as he once again demanded, "You are mine, Sadie. Say it. Mine!"

The pressure on her clit increased, forcing her over the cliff of pleasure as she screamed, "Yes…yes…yes…I am yours, Orion. YOURS!"

Flying high, Sadie had never felt anything so amazing, but just as she was sure she'd found nirvana, the shimmering grey scales of Orion's dragon covered his face and chest, his teeth grew long and sharp, and with a roar of conquest, he came inside her as his canines pierced the flesh just over her jugular.

Sadie was once again flying high. Her eyes slid shut. Fireworks danced behind her closed eyelids. She fought to breathe. Over and over she screamed Orion's name until her throat was raw and her voice but a scratchy whisper.

Floating to the earth, she felt him slide from her body before holding her to his chest, turning and laying them both down on the blanket she had no idea when he'd laid out. Giving into the pull of unconsciousness, the last thing she felt before succumbing to the darkness was Orion's chest against her back, his arm around her waist, and his lips kissing the mark she knew he'd left on her neck. Never had she felt so cherished, so protected...and so totally and completely scared out of her mind.

What have I done? Round one goes to Fate, Destiny, and the man with the bottomless blue eyes...

Chapter Six

"Tell me dragon. Tell me what I want to know and the pain will end." The monk's fetid breath beat at Orion's senses as the bastard carved at his back with a silver athame.

Biting his tongue until he tasted his own blood, Orion refused to cry out, refused to speak...refused to acknowledge the existence of his tormentors at all costs. He had lost count of the days, months, years he'd been hanging in these catacombs, tortured by religious zealots, repeatedly asked to betray not only his kin, but their heritage.

They had tried fire, knives, poisons, anything they could think of to make him give up the location of the original Cave of the Ancients. Thankfully, his grandfather was one of the original Kings and had passed not only his knowledge, but also his strength to his grandson. No matter what the monks did, the dragon of Orion's soul, the same who had lived within his grandfather, had been able to combat it with his pure white dragon magic and heal the Guardsman...at least until now.

It appeared the zealots had gotten smarter, or perhaps just lucky, by the feel of the blade presently slashing through his skin, marking him with runes. He had already scented the boiling silver, felt the heat of the fire on the backs of his legs, and knew beyond all doubt that when they were done flaying his flesh, they would be attempting to make their evil glyphs permanent with the caustic metal.

Praying to the Heavens that they were not able to disturb the marking given to him by the Universe upon his birth, the one representing the dragon with whom he shared his soul, Orion continued to stare at the wall before him and keep his lips tightly clasped. All too soon, the cutting stopped and the short, squatty monk came to stand in front of the Guardsman, his gnarled, dirty fingers digging into Orion's cheeks as he spat, "Tell me, Cretan. Tell me where to find the Cave of the Ancients and I shall end your suffering forever."

Refusing to acknowledge the zealot's presence, the Guardsman heard the shuffled footsteps approaching his back mere seconds before boiling silver was poured over his shoulders, leaving fiery trails of scorched flesh and blisters down his back, chest, and legs. Breathing slowly through his nose, staring at the same tiny spot on the wall, Orion fell so far into his own mind to escape the pain that instead of enduring the agony, he was now watching it happen, safe and secure in a world of his own making.

He smiled as both monks flew into a rage at his unresponsiveness. Laughed out loud in his own mind as one grabbed a whip, striking the sweltering skin on his back until pieces of silver-coated flesh began to fly around the dungeon as the older, taller, thinner, decrepit hooded figure cheered him on.

The sound of a wooden door scraping against the concrete floor echoed throughout the chamber as in flew the Abbot, screaming, "STOP! STOP THIS RIGHT NOW!" He tore the whip from the monk's hand and threw it against the far wall, continuing to yell, "He must NOT be harmed! We have strict orders from the Bishop to keep this abomination alive until he gives the location of the cave."

Orion watched as the man dressed in red robes as opposed to the drab brown the others wore, slapped both monks across the face, pointed at the ground, and commanded, "Kneel!"

As if their legs had fallen out from under them, the clergymen fell to their knees and stared in fear as the Abbot fetched the whip and returned to stand behind them. Without preamble, he struck first one and then the other, over and over until they were little more than sniveling, huddled masses lying on the floor in fetal positions.

Dropping the whip, the Abbot bellowed, "To the chapel! Pray for forgiveness until I come to get you!"

Ladies of the Sky

Watching the monks stumble to their feet then shuffle from the room, Orion admitted to feeling a bit of satisfaction but still remained in the part of his psyche where he felt no pain. Turning on his heels, the Abbot left without a backward glance, and slammed the door.

His vision turned dark. The Guardsman felt as though he was falling forward for several seconds, then abruptly stopped, the light immediately returning to his sight. In this scene, he was chained to the wall. No longer viewing, but once again an active participant in the nightmare. Although in the same room, he knew from the length of his hair and beard and the healed scars on his arms and legs that it was much further in the future.

He watched the Abbot preparing yet another of the herbal concoctions he believed would weaken the Guardsman enough for the zealots to finally get the information they so desperately wanted. Orion watched, and for the first time in all his years of suffering at the hands of these madmen, actually thought about telling them that if the glyphs in his back and the silver in his system hadn't weakened his resolve, nothing would. He even opened his mouth but snapped it shut in the next second, deciding it would be a waste of time and energy.

Picking yet another spot on the wall to stare at, this one his own blood, the Guardsman prepared for whatever pain was to come. He had just taken a deep breath to begin the meditation that would allow him to take the punishment while keeping his sanity when an explosion rocked the walls of the catacombs.

Racing to the door, the Abbot yelled, "Father Thomas! Father Peter!"

Only to be answered by another explosion, this one causing the steel supports used to hang the chains from the ceiling that they had utilized years earlier in his torture to fall to the stone floor with a loud crash, followed by falling rocks and rubble. Dust blocked the Guardsman's view as he listened to the Abbot continue to call out the names of his monks, his tone increasingly insistent and panicked.

By the time the third explosion rocked the building, the Abbot's screams had stopped. The huge steel hooks holding the silver chains tied around Orion's wrists, ankles, and midsection were knocked loose as half the ceiling caved in, also covering the floor in piles of stone and rubble. With a single pull, the Guardsman was able to dislodge the restraints from the wall. Dragging the chain across the stone floor, he nearly missed being crushed by yet more falling debris from the ceiling before making it into a small closet hidden under the stairs.

Tearing the caustic metal from where it had eaten through his skin and become embedded in his muscle inch by excruciating

77

inch, he listened to the footsteps of the monks who remained pounding on the floor over his head. Finally finished, blood covering every inch of his body and tattered clothing, Orion climbed out of the cupboard, over the pile of debris, and out the monstrous hole in the wall. Running as fast as he could, the Guardsman tore through the cemetery, dashed into the mausoleum and after securing the door, slid down the wall to wait until nightfall when he could begin his journey home without being seen.

Jumping from his slumber, his knife at the ready, Orion stood motionless as a doe and her fawn moved across the forest unaware and unbothered by his presence. Letting out the breath he had been holding, the Guardsman sat back down on the blanket, scrubbed his hands over his face, and noted the absence of the woman whom he'd shared one of the most important and amazing events of his life.

Shaking his head, he watched a lizard scurrying under and over the fallen leaves on the forest floor as he spoke aloud to himself. "Did you really think she was going to be here?" Pulling his shirt over his head and sliding his feet into his boots, he further scolded himself. "You should have stayed awake. Kept watch. Made sure she didn't get away."

Standing and putting on his jacket, he picked up the blanket, his excuse for being anywhere near the woman who turned his world inside-out and upside-down, folded it as compactly as he could, and leaned back against the tree that held a myriad of wonderful memories from the night before. Looking to the right and then to the left, he scented the air, immediately found the succulent aroma of apple blossoms, and smiled.

Unable to wait a moment longer, Orion took a deep breath, tucked the blanket under his arm, and headed in the direction he knew his mate had traveled. Hours passed as the sun shone high in the sky. He thought about running but was having such an enjoyable trek through the forest, looking at all the things he'd missed over the years, he couldn't bring himself to hurry.

"The longer it takes, the less likely it is that my lady love will know I am coming," he told himself. "I can just imagine the frown on her spectacularly expressive face when she sees I have once again tracked her down." He grinned as he thought aloud. "The way her brow crinkles and her eyes narrow, calling attention to the golden hues in their beautifully brown depths."

He kicked a rock and even hummed as he remembered the pink blush that covered her cheeks when she was miffed and the strong set of her shoulders when she challenged him. His mouth watered remembering the taste of her perfect lips and the feel of her soft, warm body.

Picking up the pace, he thought of making love with his dragoness every night, waking up to kiss her breathless every morning and spending the rest of his life showing her exactly what she meant to him. He thought of the life they would have. The happiness they would share and the love that would grow exponentially with each passing day fueled every step Orion took.

Lost in thought, the Guardsman missed the sudden absence of the birds overhead, the squirrels gathering their nuts, and the other sounds of the forest that had accompanied him throughout his journey. He didn't notice the broken tree branches or piles of sawdust littering the forest floor or the mound of dirt just to the left of where he walked as he daydreamed about again seeing his mate.

Picking up the pace, the Guardsman was all but jogging when he stepped forward and the ground was suddenly gone from under his feet. Falling into the darkness, opening his enhanced senses as wide as they would go, Orion dropped the woolen blanket and reached out and grabbed a thick root jutting from the walls of the hole he'd just plummeted into.

Stopping with a painful jerk, he heard the pop of a tendon and the snap of bone as his shoulder pulled from its socket. White hot pain shot through his arm and his vision blurred as the Guardsman roared in pain, holding onto the root with all his might but unable to stand the strain of his own weight upon his injuries.

Once again falling into the darkness, he landed abruptly in an icy stream of water, flowing quickly toward what sounded like underground falls. Grabbing hold of a rock with his uninjured arm, it took several tries before Orion was finally able to pull himself onto the flat surface of a much larger rock and collapse, struggling for air.

When he could finally move, the Guardsman carefully got to his feet and using the first tree he could find, forced his shoulder back into the socket with a loud pop. Dizzy from the pain, he slid down the trunk and sat as still as possible, calling upon his dragon to heal his injuries.

Almost instantaneously, he felt the warm glow of pure white dragon magic in the depths of his soul. With every breath, it filled his body, took away his pain, and began to repair his torn muscles and broken bones. Eyes heavy, his head falling back from the blessed lack of pain, and pure exhaustion, Orion had just begun to float on a cloud of unconsciousness when the barrel of a gun touched his temple and a heavily accented voice ordered, "To your feet, dragon. I don't need your brains to drink your blood."

Chapter Seven

"You what?!" Phryne screamed.

Swatting her sister on the shoulder, Sadie scolded, "Shut up, will you? Everyone will hear."

Moving her coffee out of the way and leaning closer, Phryne whispered, "Are you serious? You slept with the hunky dragon?" She waggled her eyebrows. "Al fresco? In the forest?" She patted Sadie's hand and grinned, "Way to go. It's about time you..."

"Stop right there," Sadie quickly interrupted. "Do not say that it was exactly what I needed."

"But it was," Phryne interjected with a coy look.

"Shut up. It was a mistake. I never..."

"Hey, wait a minute," Phryne slapped the table. "Did you do a shag and shoo and leave him lying in the woods?" Jumping to her feet, her sister scolded, "Oh my goddess, Sadie, you can't do that." Pointing at the door of her cottage, she ordered, "Get back out there and find him, apologize, and at least bring him back here for coffee."

"First of all, shag and shoo? Really? How long have you been holding on to that one?" Although her sister only winked over the rim of her coffee cup, Sadie knew Phryne had been saving that special little dig for an occasion just like was happening at that very moment. Leveling her gaze, she added, "And secondly, I will *not* go back and find him."

"Yes, you will," Phryne growled, leaning over Sadie, trying to be intimidating.

Slowly sliding out her chair, the dragoness got to her feet and growled, "I will not." She closed the distance between them until the tip of her nose almost touched her sister's. "It was a mistake that will *never* happen again and I am sorry I even told you."

"Dammit, Sadie! Why?' Phryne threw her hands in the air as she flopped back into her chair. Shaking her head, she glanced up with a sad pout and sighed. "Why won't you give yourself a chance to be happy?"

"Happy? Is that what you think this *man* can do for me? Who says I'm not happy right now, right here, doing what we have been doing for most of our lives?"

Shaking her head, Phryne sighed. "You know exactly what I mean. Yes, I believe you would be perfectly content to go right along living every day like you have for the last century; taking care of us while shouldering the weight of the world." She held up her index finger to stop Sadie from interrupting and continued, "But it is time for you to realize that we are all grown and more than capable of taking care of ourselves. That if you find a life of your own, you are not letting us, or the Guardian, or your parents down in any way, shape, or form." She stood and began to pace. "You are actually honoring your mom and dad by taking the wonderful life they gave you and doing something even more spectacular with it." She sat back down and Sadie followed suit. "Tell me the truth, Sadie, don't you want little dragons running all over, setting things on fire?" She grinned. "Don't you want to know what true love and fiery passion feel like, to have someone think you hung the moon and stars? For them to know all your faults and love you anyway?" She laid her hands over Sadie's and patted. "Just think of it, someone who thinks all your little quirks and weird habits are cute."

"I do not have *little quirks and weird habits*," Sadie mumbled, trying to deflect everything else her sister had said.

Sarcastically nodding her head with a wide-eyed look, Phryne held up her hands, palms out, and in an exaggerated tone said, "Yeah, okay, you keep living in La-La-Land," before laughing out loud.

Standing and walking around the table, Phryne motioned with her head and opened her arms. "Come on, give us a hug."

Begrudgingly, Sadie stood and hugged her sister. After a big embrace, complete with a kiss on the cheek, Phryne leaned back and said, "You know I love you and so do all the girls. We just want you to be happy, Sadie girl." She stepped back and dropped her arms. "Take a chance."

"You know you're the second person in as many days to tell me the same thing."

"See there. Then I have to be right, *right?*" Her sister laughed out loud.

Caught up in Phryne's infectious enthusiasm, Sadie shook her head and chuckled. "I don't know if you're right, but you are definitely persistent." Picking up her pack and bow, she added, "Now, I'm going to check the traps and see if I can get a bit of hunting in as the sun goes down. I should be back before midnight."

"Okay, be safe," Phryne said as she began clearing the table. "I'm going to weed the garden. I'll let the others know where you are if they ever get their lazy butts out of bed."

"Thanks. Talk later," the dragoness called over her shoulder as she left Phryne's cottage and headed off to the other side of the forest, absolutely positive the presence of Orion had scared away most of the game.

"If he's even still there," she mused to herself, moving quickly through the forest. As she followed the convoluted, strategic trail that led to the traps that provided she and her clan with food, Sadie did everything in her power not to think about that damned man or what they shared.

Over and over she told herself it didn't matter what Fate wanted, that she was the master of her own Destiny and had been since she was five years old. She was Scathach Sorcha Ashford, Rightful Leader of the Mighty Ashford Dragons and the Clan of the Lady Flyers. Her life was full and she had no time for anything or *anyone* else.

But then she would remember what it felt like to be in Orion's arms, to have him declaring over and over that she was *his*, making her acknowledge their connection, making her feel things she never thought possible. She couldn't deny how right it felt to surrender to another, to know there was someone else in the world with whom she shared an undefinable, unexplainable bond, completing her in ways she hadn't even known were missing until he appeared. It was freeing to have him take control, to not think about who needed what or where she needed to be. To just be in the moment and feel the incredible emotions that one man, one special dragon, could wring out of her. He was strong and domineering but in the kindest and gentlest of ways, a true enigma that, if she was completely honest with herself, she really did want to get to know better.

No sooner had the thought crossed her mind than all her old insecurities and doubts reared their ugly heads. How could she love him as she knew he would demand, completely and totally without reservation, giving all that she was and accepting the same from him, knowing there was a real chance he would leave or die or Heavens forbid, be taken again? Could she suffer another loss like that of her parents or the Guardian? If she surrendered to the feelings growing within not only her, but also her dragon, and something was to happen that separated them from Orion and his beast, would she be strong enough to live without his love until it was her time to join him in the Heavens?

Sadie just didn't have all the answers and *that*, above all else, bothered her the most. It was unfamiliar and uncomfortable territory and to quote her sister, Daphne, a Hoopoe shifter with the powers of healing, water divination, incredible intuition, and the youngest among them... 'it just plain sucked.'

Smiling to herself, Sadie laughed out loud when she thought of how quick-witted, funny, and free-spirited Daphne was despite looking like Snow White in human form and a raven on steroids with her feathers on. Between her and Pearl, there was no secret that could be kept and very few surprises.

Except me having a mate who basically fell from the sky...

The questions just kept flowing as she made her way to her favorite hunting spot. Climbing the ancient Ash, reaching the center of the tree, more than halfway up its nearly eighty-foot height, hidden by the plethora of leaves and branches, the dragoness sat, thinking and wishing there was an off switch for her brain.

With less than an hour until sundown, Sadie tried to think about anything but Orion; however, the harder she tried to fill her mind with something...*anything else*, the more her thoughts revolved around one very sexy, very persistent male dragon. Several times as the sky turned from brilliant blue to a myriad of pinks and purples and the sun moved farther toward the horizon, the dragoness was sure she heard his voice, but after scenting the air and reaching out with her preternatural senses, she found nothing and chalked it up to her overactive imagination.

Finally, darkness descended upon the forest. Sadie sat at the ready, her bow in her hands, an arrow across her lap. Just as she had predicted, ten or so deer wandered out of the cover of the brambles at the edge of the woods and walked to the lake bank. It was heartwarming to watch the mothers making sure their fawns got enough to drink before they even thought about taking care of themselves.

And just like that, the image of smoldering azure eyes and alluring masculinity made her body warm as a perfect image of Orion's face appeared in her mind. This time, however, she pictured the children Phryne had mentioned earlier in the day. Little girls with bright blue eyes, long pewter curls, and an adoration for their father that was boundless, closely followed by rambunctious boys with smiling brown eyes and wavy brown locks, who only had eyes for their momma.

I have lost my mind…that is the only explanation…

No sooner had she deemed herself ready to live alone on a hill with a sign that read *Enter at Own Risk, Crazy Old Dragon Lady Lives Here*, Sadie caught sight of a ten-point buck striding from the opposite side of the lake. He called to his herd, announcing his arrival just as two more smaller, younger males galloped to catch up.

Sliding the bow string into the nock of her arrow, Sadie placed the shaft on the arrow rest then pulled the string taut before sighting in the smallest of the bucks. Waiting patiently for the deer to raise his head, allowing her to make the perfect shot, the dragoness counted backward as her father taught her all those years ago.

Ten...nine...eight... The words floated through her mind as she sat unmoving, not breathing, waiting for the perfect shot.

Seven...six...five... The largest buck raised his majestic head, looked left then right, then began following the doe and their fawns.

Four...Three...Two... The two remaining males finally looked up, called to their herd, and began galloping just as Orion's agonizing roar burst through her mind.

"Go ahead and kill me! I'll never tell you where she is!"

Chapter Eight

"Orion? Is that you?"

Sadie's voice cut through the relentless monologue of the masked man brandishing the red-hot branding iron. The Shadow could only assume that the combination of his fury and need to protect his mate had finally forced their mental connection, for he hadn't been able to use his mind speak in any capacity since his initial capture over a century ago.

"You *will* tell me what I want to know, dragon." The maniac's voice was heavily accented, reminding Orion of the short time he and the lads had spent in the Orient. "Female dragons are rare, indeed. Actually, I had been told they were extinct." He shoved the tip of the iron bar into the fire roaring before Orion. "While the restorative powers of your heart and blood and the meal of your bones will sustain me for decades, the same from a female who still possesses the ability to reproduce will not only allow me to live for centuries, but, it is my understanding, that it will repair the damage inflicted by others of your kind."

The masked freak pulled the branding iron from the fire, gazed at the glowing metal for several long seconds, and then with a speed Orion hadn't expected, jabbed it into the Guardsman's stomach. Gritting his teeth, refusing to cry out as pain ravaged his midsection, the scent of burning flesh filled his senses and his dragon roared with the need to avenge the man with whom he shared his soul.

When his masked captor finally pulled the branding iron away, Orion used every ounce of his considerable strength not to pass out or even lean forward from where he was chained against a cold, stone wall. Any sign of weakness would be considered a victory by the masked maniac before him, one he would use to his deranged advantage. The Guardsman had learned long ago how to endure torture. The only difference now was that he was no longer alone. If Sadie could hear him, maybe his brethren could, too. His only concern was the magic filling the chamber where he was being held.

Could the masked maniac before him also tap into his mental communication with those he called family? It was a chance the Guardsman was not willing to take. Orion would bide his time, wait until the freak left the room, and then attempt to contact Drago and the others. Until then, he tuned back into the fanatic's ramblings, listening for clues as to his name or where he was holding the Guardsman.

Waving the branding iron like a prop, the masked maniac lectured, "I am sure you do not remember me, Orion McKendrick, formerly of the Grey Dragon Clan and later the Enforcers, but we have most assuredly met before."

There was no time to be shocked at the maniac's revelation, although Orion had no doubt it was the main reason he, above all the other dragons in the world, had been targeted. No, the fact that his captor knew him only extenuated the fact that the dragon needed to figure out who he was and how to escape swiftly. The Guardsman had to make sure the madman before him was annihilated before the fanatic sent any of the many people Orion could sense mulling around wherever he was being held to capture Sadie.

Pacing back and forth, the masked maniac tapped the end of the iron poker against the stone floor with every other step. Orion took note of the slight limp in his left leg, the way his right arm hung at an odd angle, and his hooked and knotted gnarled fingers bouncing against his leg as he walked. The madman's hair was more white than black but still very thick and stick straight, the end touching the tops of his shoulders, held back by the black leather cord that secured the ominous silver mask to his face.

"Think back, if you will." The masked man stopped directly in front of Orion, turned, walked closer, and leaned forward until mere inches separated them. As he spoke, the Guardsman got his first up close look at the silver mask covering his face.

Its birdlike features were incredibly exaggerated, reminding Orion of a statue he had seen while in Japan. He searched his memories, using the small, intricately designed comb bisecting the skull, the small ringed eyes, the waddle under its chin, and the snoods on either side of its very pronounced, very wide beak to call up all he could remember of that time so long ago. He saw delicately carved anti-Buddhism runes hidden within the etched feathers decorating the edges that were the closest to his captor's ears as he sifted through his memories while also listening to the mad man before him.

"To a time when you and your Force, as I believe you call them, were called to assist the Golden Dragons of Tokyo. Although not of your bloodline or sect, still distant kin and therefore, yours to protect and help."

With no warning, the madman jammed the pointed side of the branding iron into the top of Orion's foot. The coppery sweet scent of his own blood and the eerie sound of cracking bones and tearing muscle filled the chamber as the Guardsman crushed his lips together to keep from screaming while his captor continued to speak.

"Do you remember that time? Do you remember the devastation and destruction you and yours rained down upon a small village of innocents in your pursuit to conquer the U~izādo threatening *your kind*?"

He twisted the thick iron poker still imbedded in Orion's foot as he spat. "Do you, abomination? Do you remember the little humans you slaughtered in the name of *your justice*?"

Pushing past the pain, returning to that part of his mind he'd been forced to use so very often during his torture at the hands of the monks, Orion let go of the pain, the fury, his worry over Sadie, and focused on replaying everything that had occurred during that specific mission. He remembered being called by Hachiro, the eighth son of the Golden Dragon King, Daichi. Drago had given Orion the go ahead to speak to the sea dragon and assess whether the Enforcers could be of any assistance.

"Tell me the situation and leave nothing out," Orion directed.

"All seven of my brothers, along with my father, my uncles, and my cousins, all but myself, the women, and the children, have been taken by the U~izādo. This ancient coven of wizards believes that by drinking the blood of a dragon and ingesting the meal of his bones they can achieve eternal life."

"They what? Is that true?"

Ladies of the Sky

"It is recorded in the history of our people but until now, my father, his Elders, and my older brothers believed only we, the nation of Japanese dragons, possessed this knowledge," Hachiro stated, fear and anger intermingling in his tone.

"And how do you know that the wizards have obtained this information? They could just be working with others of your enemies to destroy their largest opposition?" Orion knew his conversation with the Japanese water dragon sounded like an interrogation, but he had to be sure to collect all the facts before making a decision that could potentially take them halfway around the world for only the Heavens knew how long.

"Last night, I disguised myself in the robes of the U~izādo and using herbs to mask my scent, followed a group of them to the outskirts of their encampment on Mount Maehotakadake in the Hida Mountains Range on the banks of the Azusa River. Using my dragon's smallest form, I traveled underwater and, while resting in the shallows, listened as their leader told them of the preparations being made to exsanguinate and dissect my clan."

"I applaud your courage and ingenuity." Orion knew his Japanese brethren appreciated being acknowledged for their achievements, especially when they were young. He could hear the trepidation and fear in the voice of Daichi's eighth and

96

youngest son and wanted to reassure the lad that he had done the right thing. They were going to need his help sooner rather than later. Orion then asked, "And when are they to carry out this plan?"

"At precisely four a.m., the hour of the dragon according to the Buddhist Patrons, on Tsukimi, the fifteenth day of the eighth month when the Harvest Moon is full in the sky and all we are to eat and drink for the next year is blessed by Siddhārtha Gautama, the Buddha himself, from his place among the stars."

"So, we have exactly seven days before the ceremony, is that right?"

"Hai," Hachiro quickly answered to the affirmative.

"How many wizards in total?"

"I counted a hundred including their leader and believe there were at least fifty more guarding my clan."

"I see," Orion thought for a moment than asked, "How many dragons? Are they all in fighting shape?" He needed to know how many would be available to exterminate the U~izādo after freeing the Golden Dragons.

"Hai," Hachiro again was quick to answer.

Orion could feel the younger dragon's anticipation through their mind-to-mind connection as he waited for the grey dragon's decision.

Taking only a moment to think, the Guardsman pushed an abundance of confidence through his connection to the sea dragon as he said, "We will take flight this evening and see you by lunchtime tomorrow. I have pulled the location of your lair from your thoughts. We will land in the valley about three miles from you and come into your clan's lands on foot."

"Arigatōgozaimashita, Masutādoragon. You and your dōhō are truly as great as the legends say. Not only will my clan owe you a meiyo no shakkin, but I also will forever be at the ready for your call, should you have need of assistance."

Smiling at being called a Master Dragon, Orion acknowledged Hachiro's honorable words the way he had been taught by the Elders, "Thank you, Hachiro. It is our honor to help such a revered and righteous clan. A Debt of Honor is not necessary as we lend our assistance out of fealty and kinship."

"The debt stands, Masutādoragon Orion, for only the strength of the Enforcers can defeat such a foe."

"We accept with great honor, Hachiro," Orion said. "We will see you very soon."

"Arigatōgozaimashita, Masutādoragon. May the wind be at your back, Fate lift your wings, and Destiny guide your journey. Until then, Sayōnara."

Orion's memories fast forwarded to the battle. The U~izādo that were able to escape during the initial infiltration had hidden in the nearby village, slaughtering the villagers and using their clothing and homes as cover.

After searching the huts and fields, the Enforcers, along with the rescued Golden Dragons, headed back to the U~izādo's encampment to destroy any and all remnants of the evil coven. Walking side-by-side with Hachiro, Orion stopped short when the young Golden Dragon turned and ran after a so-called farmer, tackling him to the ground and ripping the sleeve from his smock.

Pointing at a tattoo of an upside-down Pentagram over the Endless Knot, the symbol of the black magic wizards, on the arm of one of the so-called farmers, Hachiro sounded the alarm. Within minutes, the remaining wizards were killed, their bodies burnt, and their ashes strewn to the four corners of the sea, along with their evil compatriots.

Racing forward, Orion's recollections then revealed the tall stone statue of a Karura. He could see the plaque at the base of the sculpture as if he were back there once again. Reading the words, he suddenly remembered why this particular being from Japanese history had fascinated him so.

The inscription read, *"Here stands a mighty Karura, one of the divine races of fire-breathing demi-gods. With the head and wings of an eagle atop its human warrior's body, Karura are fearsome. Not only do they breathe fire from their beaks, but the flapping of their wings sounds like thunder and the gusts of wind they create are so strong that they protect the Rulers and their families from heavy rains and typhoons. Their venom can cure poison and disease and they feast upon the flesh of dragons and water serpents.*

A Karura can only be killed by a dragon of pure heart, wearing a Buddhist talisman and firing a Hōzen, a sacred arrow carved from a Yōryū Tree, into the center of the creature's heart by the dragon's right hand. The destruction of this divine being can only be considered when the Karura has turned its eyes from the light and is endangering the blessed people of the Buddha."

Yanked from his memories as punishing, burning, mind-bending pain shot through his foot, up his leg, and made it hard for him to breathe from the masked maniac pulling the iron poker from his flesh, Orion seethed through gritted teeth, "Dragons did *not* harm any humans in the battle against the U~izādo. That guilt and the dishonor of those deaths lay squarely at the feet of those demon-worshipping, black-magic wielding wizards, you spineless piece of shit."

The words had barely crossed his lips before his captor swung the branding iron like a baseball bat firmly connecting with Orion's ribs. Once again the sound of bones crushing filled the chamber immediately followed by the roar of pure agony as the Guardsman could no longer hold back his anguish.

Flipping his mask off with such force it banged and clanged against the far wall before falling to the stone floor and breaking into several large pieces that glimmered in the still roaring firelight, the madman roared. Grabbing Orion's face and squeezing it to the point of pain between his thumb and forefinger, the grotesque figure before him spat, "You lie, abomination!"

As the freak held Orion's face, his hand shaking with rage, spittle running down his skeletal chin, it felt as if the maniac's cataract-clouded eyes were trying to bore a hole in the Guardsman's skull as he added, "I was *there*. I saw what you *winged lizards* did to my family, my friends, everyone and everything I had ever known."

Orion could barely stand to look at his sallow skin as it slid from his skull like melting wax. His lips curled in the most unnatural of ways, making the maniac look as if he had a permanent scowl and showcasing his black and rotted teeth. If what the freak was saying was the truth, he had been alive for over a century and was showing every single second of it.

Opening his mouth to retaliate, the Guardsman's jaw snapped shut when the maniac flung the dragon's head back against the stone wall and screeched, "I was there, dammit! I saw what you and your kind did to my people." He slapped Orion so hard the Guardsman's ears rang as he bellowed, "And you shall pay!"

Grabbing Orion by the hair while shaking his already battered skull until the Shadow saw double, the maniac whispered, "I *am* Karura. I have only to drink your blood, eat your bones and that of your mate's, and I shall live forever."

Karura let Orion's head fall forward before adding with an evil chuckle, "Never fear, abomination, I found you when the monks had you and you know what happened to them. Before I am through with you, you will tell me where to find that pretty little female of yours. Of that you can be certain."

Chapter Nine

"Orion, I swear to the Heavens I will skin you myself if you don't answer me."

Sadie had been issuing threats and tracking the male dragon's scent for nearly three hours in the complete darkness of the forest. Walking around in circles, finding little more than Orion's footsteps in the erratic and chaotic trail she believed was at least partially false, the dragoness was just about to call upon her sisters when she stepped upon an especially soft pile of fallen leaves and broken branches.

Using her enhanced senses, the princess inspected the debris and found a six-foot by four-foot rectangle of new grass hidden under the clippings. Scooping away the leaves to get a closer look at what someone obviously had tried to hide, Sadie used the blade of her knife to raise a corner. Catching a glimpse of something shiny, the dragoness kept peeling back the section of new grass until she revealed a steel trap door locked tight with not only a huge electronic silver combination lock, but also a bit of nasty magic.

"And just what are you hiding under here?" she asked the darkness. "A dragon, maybe?"

Ladies of the Sky

Sitting crossed legged beside the door, Sadie studied its hinges and the mechanism keeping it secure, because she had the strangest feeling that the mysticism she felt would stun not only her, but also her dragon. Pulling the jeweled dagger the Guardian had given to the dragoness before surrendering to the cancer ravaging her body, the princess studied the inscription on its blade, shining bright despite the darkness. *Blessed by the holy, held by the loved, wielded by the faithful.*

Touching the pendant that hung around her neck and looking at the ring on her finger, she thought about that fateful day when she, a ten-year little girl, was playing behind the two-story home that housed the seven female shifters under the Guardian's care. Sadie remembered the tall thin man, dressed completely in black except for his red plaid muffler, wearing a stove-pipe hat and carrying a small blue box with a jeweled lock.

"Are you Princess Scathach Sorcha Ashford, Royal and Rightful Leader of the Mighty Ashford Dragons?" His voice was gravelly and breathy. His face pale and wrinkled.

Standing tall, she rolled her shoulders back and answered as she'd been taught. "Yes, my good sir, I am. How may I or any of my clan be of assistance?"

The man smiled, his watery-blue eyes sparkling with delight as he took her outstretched hand, kissed her tiny ruby ring, and nodded, "It is I, Gabriel Gustafson of the Guardians' Guild who is here to be of service to you." Standing back to his full height, Gabriel continued, "May I accompany you inside and speak with you in the presence of your Guardian?"

This Guardian was the first she'd ever met with a name. All the others had always simply been called, Guardian. It intrigued Sadie, as well as did his easy demeanor and quick smile. Motioning as she turned, the princess smiled, "Yes, of course. Follow me."

Entering the house, she called for her Guardian before turning to Gabriel and offering, "Would you like some tea, Mr. Gustafson?"

"No, but thank you very much, princess." He followed her into the living room. "If we can just sit here and talk, that would be most accommodating."

Barely sitting down before her Guardian entered the room, Sadie sat tall with her hands folded across her lap and her ankles crossed, just as her mother had taught her. She waited until everyone was seated and then asked, "Now, Mr. Gustafson, what is it that you have for me?"

She glanced at the box on his lap and waited patiently as he looked at her Guardian and then at her before beginning to speak. His voice was lower than it had been previously, his mouth downturned and his eyes no longer sparkling as he said, "It is with a heavy heart and immense sadness that I come here today to tell you that your mother and father, Elder and Lady Ashford, the Royal and Rightful Leaders of the Ashford Dragons, have been killed in battle."

Gabriel stood, placed the blue box on the couch next to her, and knelt before her with his head bowed. "Here are the belongings they have left to you, as well as their last decree that you, Princess Scathach Sorcha Ashford and your true fated mate, shall lead the Ashford Dragons and your descendants after you and theirs, after them, and so on until the end of time."

Standing, he then touched the top of her head and said in the language of dragon kin, "Beo fada, grá maith agus ag eitilt ard."

She felt the magic he was imparting to her, as she answered, "Thank you, Guardian. I will do my utmost to live as long as the Universe has need of me, love as well as my parents before me and their parents before them, and fly as high as the sky allows, with the sun to guide my path."

"You will make an excellent Leader, Sadie Ashford. You have the strength of your ancestors to see you through whatever life has planned. I look forward to witnessing your great deeds."

Shaking herself out of her memories, she chuckled sarcastically, "Oh, Gabriel, if you could only see me now."

Focusing on what she knew she had to do and having never taken the time to learn spells, Sadie began to use what the Guardian had called Thought Mysticism and pulled up an image of Orion. She saw him peacefully sleeping on his side, a slight smile gracing his perfect lips as the first rays of the sun had just started to break through the leaves of the trees overhead. It was awe-inspiring how the ruggedly handsome and immensely strong man could also be gentle and loving. Although he scared the living daylights out of her, the dragoness had to admit, at least to herself, that she truly did want to get to know him better.

"So, that means I have to go and save his mangy butt."

She chewed on her bottom lip as she focused even harder on the thought of Orion. A warm, pure light shone in her heart. It moved slowly but steadily through her body to her soul, making every doubt and fear she had seem manageable. If Sadie knew anything, it was that accepting whatever life had to throw at her was just part of the game. She wasn't ready to jump on board with the whole mating thing, but she knew if both she and Orion lived through whatever was about to happen, she would have to at least hear him out.

Slowly sliding the Guardian's blade across her palm, Sadie thought only of Orion, the night they had shared and that a world without him would simply be incomplete and lacking. Squeezing her fist, she watched as drops of her blood dripped onto the mechanized lock, popping and fizzing like drops of water on a hot griddle.

Telling the dragon of her soul to hold back her healing power, Sadie slowly drew a line around the lock and across all three hinges in her life's essence, watching as it literally ate holes in the metal, culminating in a loud pop and the door being flung several feet away. Looking into the darkness, thankful for her enhanced vision, she saw a metal staircase leading farther into the depths than even she could see.

Standing, she put her pack on her shoulder, the Guardian's blade in the holster at her waist, and the sword she'd laid on the ground by her hip in the scabbard across her back. It felt strange not to take her bow but knew it was best to leave it in the tree. Where she was headed was going to require up-close-and-personal hand-to-hand combat.

Taking a deep breath, she touched the pendant that hung between her breasts and looked at the ring on her finger. Thinking back to that blue box Gabriel Gustafson had given her all those years ago and the treasures of her parent's favorite pieces of jewelry, she took her first step into the darkness, whispering, "Okay, Orion, since you won't answer me, I'm coming to find you, *then* I'm going to kick your butt myself."

The farther she descended into the black, inky underground, the louder the sound of flowing water became, the cooler the air felt, and the stronger she could scent Orion's blood. She had already masked her scent with the herbs the Guardian had taught her to use and also some that Pearl prepared after her recent trip to the Orient.

Letting her enhanced senses loose, Sadie counted ten strong human heartbeats, one very sluggish one, and one that beat with the vigor of a dragon. As she stepped off the bottom step, the heel of her boot sank into the damp soil of the riverbed she'd been listening to. Looking around, she asked herself, "How have I lived here all these years and not known any of this existed? Either someone is good at hiding or my clan and myself have grown complacent." Now irritated with herself, she huffed, "When I get out of here, I'm having Daphne and Pearl set up wards to cover the whole damned forest."

She watched the water careening toward a bed of rocks where it splashed up and over the stones creating white caps on its way to what she was sure was a waterfall of quite some height. Beautiful orange, white, and black scales of a school of koi fish glittered under the running stream as they gulped at the algae that floated along the edge of the brook. Watching the koi, Sadie was able to judge where the current of the water was the weakest and with three quick strides, crossed the stream and slid further into the lush greenery.

Sufficiently hidden, she moved stealthily through the man-made jungle until the vegetation began to thin out and she could hear the voices of the men whose heartbeats she'd heard during her descent. Kneeling behind a fake rock that she knew was hiding something electronic from the buzzing she picked up with her sensitive hearing and the vibrations she felt under her knees, Sadie listened as four of the heartbeats moved closer to where she sat with two others about fifty feet behind them and another pair a hundred feet behind them. Pushing a bit farther, she found the last two much farther back but less than twenty feet from the sluggish heartbeat which was right next to Orion.

"Guess the baddie has a bad heart," she sighed under her breath. "Won't be a problem for long."

Taking a deep breath, she kissed her mother's ring and touched her father's pendant before letting out the breath she'd just taken as the first guard's foot touched down next to her knee. Almost quicker than even her own eye could track, Sadie sliced the tendons in the back of both his ankles and the ones of the

110

guard behind him before rolling between their falling bodies, jumping to her feet, and stabbing the other two men in the heart who were turning toward her trying to grab their guns.

Quickly hiding the dead bodies behind the fake rock, the dragoness waited next to them for the next two guards, disposing of them in quite the same fashion before jogging along the riverbank until she could see the guards outside a set of twelve-foot stainless steel double doors. Watching them standing there completely still, breathing so slowly it took her enhanced eyesight to see the rise and fall of their chests, Sadie zeroed in on their strong, steady heartbeats, glad to see she'd made as far as she had undetected.

Creeping closer, she was just about to make her move when Orion's voice burst through her mind, this time not in pain but in a tone that made her think about leaving him to suffer. *"Sadie, please tell me you are not outside the door. Do you not have one iota of self-preservation anywhere in that beautiful head of yours?"*

Chapter Ten

He could feel her anger, knew he had caused it, and figured maybe she had a right. He had opened his mouth and inserted both his size twelves before thinking it through, but in his defense, he'd been speaking out of fear and the overwhelming need to protect his mate. Karura wanted Sadie above all others and, dammit all, if she wasn't playing right into his hands.

Orion was just about to explain himself when his mate's normally sultry, now surly, voice growled, *"I could ask you the same thing, but from the smell of your blood decorating every inch of whatever little piece of hell you discovered, I already know the answer is a resounding no. So, keep your mouth shut and let me rescue you. We can debate the finer points of my plan later."*

Had silver not been eating away at his flesh and a madman planning to drink not only his blood and eat his bones but those of his lovely Sadie as well, Orion might have laughed out loud at his mate's sass and courage. However, he wanted her out of the immediate vicinity as fast as her feet would carry her. *"Sadie,"* he barked. *"You* have *to go. You don't understand. This bastard is not easy to kill and* you *are the one he wants. I am just the bait."*

There was no response. Absolutely nothing....just dead air.

He could feel her. Knew she was there. Was sure she had heard him, but also felt her resentment at his words and her incredible determination to do whatever it took to free him and kill the man responsible for his suffering. He applauded her resolve, was hopeful that she was finally accepting him as her mate, was thrilled that she cared enough to come for him, but the fact remained that he *needed* her to leave...*had* to know that she was safe.

"Sadie...Sadie, answer me."

"I'm a little busy here," she ground out through gritted teeth just as Orion heard two bodies hit the floor outside the massive door to his right, one right after another like dominoes.

"I guess..."

The Guardsman's words were cut off as Sadie burst through the huge steel doors sword swinging at precisely the same second Karura jammed the thickest needle Orion had ever seen into his jugular and began drinking the dragon's blood as it poured from the attached tubing. Struggling against his bonds while watching the greatest enemy he had ever faced literally healing and growing stronger before his eyes, the Guardsman felt as helpless as a small child.

Raising his head, Karura now looked almost human as he licked Orion's bright red blood from his shriveled, scarred lips. The stench of the bastard's breath, now tinged with the sweet, coppery scent of the dragon's life essence, stung the Guardsman's nose as the demented creature screamed, "Guards! Guards! Take the female! Kill the male, if you have to, but she," he pointed right at Sadie, "is not to be harmed."

Karura's minions, dressed in white from head-to-toe with only their eyes showing, poured in from an overhead door at the rear of the cavern Orion hadn't seen until just that moment. His eyes searched the sea of snowy enemies until they landed on his beautiful mate, taking on all opponents, stopping at nothing to arise the victor and save not only the day, but his sorry dragon ass.

His Sadie was poetry in motion. The raw power contained in every strike of her sword and slash of her jeweled dagger was like a perfectly choreographed ballet. She swung and kicked, spun and sliced her way through all comers, decorating their milky uniforms with blood and gore, creating an impressionistic masterpiece like she was the artist and they her blank canvas.

Never, in all the battles, in all his years as a Guardsman, had Orion witnessed anything like his dragoness protecting what was hers. Watching the last of the guards fall to the stony floor, both man and dragon had just let out the breath they had been holding when the sound of clanking armor and movement out of the corner of Orion's eye drew their attention.

Screaming, *"Sadie!"* directly into her mind as Orion took in Karura marching into the chamber covered in the gleaming gold-plated Japanese samurai style armor, the dragon knew his heart skipped at least two beats. A mask reminiscent of the first, still birdlike but more ornate, with two ivory horns carved to dangerous points on either side of the attached helmet and a row of thin metal spikes bisecting his skull and ending at his chainmail neckpiece, was just the beginning. Searching for any weaknesses, Orion could see his mate doing the same thing in her mind.

Either stress, fear, pain, pride in his beautiful dragoness, or some combination thereof, had forced the missing pieces of the bond growing between he and Sadie into place. Not only could he speak directly into her mind, but now he could feel what she was feeling, hear what she was thinking, see what she saw, and recognize the light in her soul as the affection she had for him taking hold and growing stronger with every beat of her heart.

Although thrilled to know she was coming to care for him, Orion forced those feelings to the side as he instructed, *"Aim for*

115

under the arm plates. The lungs or the arteries on the underside of his arms will incapacitate him almost immediately."

"Is that so?" Sadie growled, her tone thick with sarcasm and her right eyebrow arched high. *"This is not my first fight with a tyrannical maniac."*

No sooner had the words entered Orion's mind than Karura pulled two thin katanas from the sheaths on his thighs, swung them with deadly accuracy, and threatened, "I don't want to kill you, my sweet, but I have no problem teaching you a lesson in obedience."

"Obedience? Is that what you're calling your brand of insanity these days?"

Karura took two long side-steps, swinging his swords in a series of overhead cuts that slashed X's in the air in front of him as he growled, "Should not a warrior as great as yourself see the defeat before her and lay down her sword.".

Sadie mirrored his movements then countered, "Honor until death. Is that not the way of the samurai?"

Her words struck a chord. The blades of Karura's swords clanged together and his hands slid on the grips. Trying to cover his blunder with bravado, the maniac growled, "What does an abomination such as you know of honor?"

Stepping closer as she once again imitated Karura's sidesteps, Orion was speechless at his mate's complete lack of fear and incredible confidence as she scoffed, "An abomination?" She rolled her wrist, spinning her sword in a perfect circle then holding it at the ready. "Is it not this abomination's blood you wish to drink? Bones you wish to ground into meal and feast upon?"

She stepped even closer, closing in on the maniac who still stayed the course; not advancing, simply posturing. "I see through your mask," Sadie snickered, taunting Karura. "See all your men...well, saw," She let a chuckle sneak out while sliding her eyes to the side, calling attention to the fifteen or so men who had met their demise at the end of her blade. "Those who blindly followed you on your ill-fated quest for immortality."

Taking another step to the side, Sadie forced Karura to also move or be close enough for her to strike. Barking out a single laugh as the masked maniac almost tripped to get away from her, Orion's mate went on, "What is it? Your momma not love you? Your daddy too tough on you?"

She pushed her bottom lip out in an over-exaggerated faux pout. "Have a big brother who bullied you?" Leaning forward as the air in the chamber was filled with the fiery scent of fury and the burnt aroma of vengeance combining with a strong overriding stench of fear that stung Orion's nose like rotten fruit as Karura's emotions began to get the best of him, Sadie taunted, "You know what I think, you masked freak of nature? I think you are just a scared little boy trying to prove he is not the washed-up loser everyone always said he would be."

Karura's battle cry combined with the echo of Sadie's derisions as he rushed forward, slicing and slashing like a madman, screeching, "You dare speak of my family?" as he thrust his blade at Sadie's chest.

Easily blocking his ill-placed strike, the dragoness lunged forward with her left foot while shoving her blade through the leather covering his right side. Pulling her blade back, she grinned as Karura wailed in pain. Although she'd missed anything vital, Orion still cheered as a crimson stain spread across the soft material of his armor.

"You over-grown lizard!" Karura spat, lunging forward and slashing with both blades, roaring as one made contact with Sadie's mid-section and blood flowed from the slash in her leather vest.

"Sadie!" Orion bellowed, pulling at his restraints, the silver cutting through the muscles and grinding against his bones as he watched her fight back, thrusting and striking the armor-clad madman in quick succession, driving Karura back, step by doggedly determined step.

Orion saw the lines near her eyes and mouth from the pain tearing through her body, but still his dragoness battled on. Sadie was magnificent. She was spectacular. She was *his*…and there was no way as long as blood flowed through his veins he was going to let her fight alone.

With pure agony wracking his bruised and beaten body, the Guardsman continued to fight against the chains and shackles holding him back. He needed to get to his mate, needed to fight by her side…needed to save her, in order to save himself.

It was then that Orion remembered the inscription on the bottom of the Karura statue he had seen all those years ago… *A Karura can only be killed by a dragon of pure heart wearing a Buddhist talisman and firing a Hōzen, a sacred arrow carved from a Yōryū Tree, into the center of the creature's heart by the dragon's right hand.*

From one heartbeat to another, as his beast forced a massive surge of pure, white dragon magic into his veins, the Shadow summoned every ounce of strength and power both man and dragon possessed and forced his body away from the wall. With a mighty roar, he pulled the bolt and hooks holding his restraints from the wall. Tearing the chains and cuffs from his flesh, Orion bellowed into Sadie's mind, *"He possesses the spirit of the Karura. You have to have a Buddhist Talisman to kill him."*

Unable to answer, Orion saw Sadie continue to batter Karura with one crushing strike of her sword and dagger after another. Stepping over the pile of silver he had just removed from his body, the Guardsman saw the bird-like mask fly from the madman's face. Watched as his dragoness cut away the huge metal breastplate from his armor and nearly jumped with joy as she jabbed both of her blades into his lungs.

Karura went down as Sadie pulled her sword and dagger from his body and stepped back, looking at Orion. But just as the Shadow had thought, the maniac was not mortally wounded. Bellowing his mate's name as Karura jumped to his feet, Orion struggled to reach Sadie as the scene before him immediately began to play out in slow motion.

Karura lunged forward, slashing a bloody X across Sadie's back. Ignoring her injuries, the dragoness spun to her left, kicked out with her right foot, and followed through with a thrust of her sword that perforated Karura's chest, passed through his heart, and pushed out his back. Moving so quickly she was but a blur, Orion's mate raced behind the madman, now on his knees, grabbed a fistful of his long grey hair, pulled his head back, and with deadly accuracy, sliced across his neck.

Dropping the dagger as blood spurted from Karura's neck, Sadie roared with all the power of both woman and dragon and yanked the madman's head from his neck, held it up, and turned toward Orion. Covered in not only her own blood but that of their enemies, his miraculous mate pulled a chain from under her ruined vest with her free hand and smiled. "Guess it is a good thing my father left me this," as she threw Karura's head atop his corpse.

Taking the last two steps that separated them as he looked at the opal pendant engraved with an Endless Knot hanging from her elegant fingers, Orion pulled Sadie to him, and as his lips touched hers in a passionate affirmation of their lives, he chuckled into her mind, *It is a damn good thing.*

Chapter Eleven

Lifting her lips from Orion's, Sadie looked at the arrogant, headstrong, domineering, absolutely fantastic dragon hellbent on worming his way into her life and everything simply fell into place. Well, maybe not *everything*, but most definitely the huge piece of her heart and soul that had been missing for as long as she could remember.

It had taken almost losing him to face one basic fact. It did not matter one iota if she needed him in her life, she *wanted* him there…right beside her, every day from now until the end of all time. They were stronger together, better together, just more…*everything* when they were together. She had been forced to accept the future the Universe, Fate, and that old bastard Destiny had intended for her.

The realization that it didn't make her weak or needy or any less of a woman, a person, a leader, or a warrior, hit her over the head like a ton of bricks the second she burst into that blasted dungeon and saw Orion chained to a wall. There had only been one decision. Fight like bloody hell to free him and never ever let him go again.

"What are you thinking so hard about, *mo dragoness álainn?*" Orion chuckled, kissing her cheek.

Waiting until he was looking her in the eye, Sadie coyly replied, "Well, if you must know, I was thinking how thankful I am that you tried to return my blanket."

Throwing back his head, Orion barked with laughter. "Now, how about that? Who would've ever thought?"

Doubling up her fist, Sadie pretended to beat her dragon in the chest as she teased, "You better watch it, bub?"

"Or what?"

"Or I might just make you hang out with me forever."

Slamming his lips to hers, Sadie gasped as Orion sighed directly into her mind, *"Deal, mo ghrá."*

Moments later, breathless and wanting nothing more than to leave the death and destruction of Karura's underground lair, Sadie stepped back and looked around. "I guess we better get rid of all this." She motioned at the bodies strewn around the chamber's stone floor.

"Right you are, *mo chroí.*"

Sadie reached out as Orion stepped on his left leg and lurched forward. Looking down, she gasped at the huge gaping wound where he literally pulled the silver chain from his leg and the hole in his foot. "You need to sit down. I can do this."

Gently laying his thumb and forefinger on either side of her chin, Orion turned her face toward his and shook his head. "*We can do this…together.*" He kissed her quickly as she started to argue, pulling back and adding, "Never alone…not anymore…deal?"

Smiling despite the situation, Sadie relented. "Deal."

Wrapping her arm around her mate's waist, she insisted he lean on her and together, as the couple she was truly beginning to believe they were supposed to be, Sadie and Orion called forth their dragon fire and incinerated the bodies of not only Karura, but also all his minions. Leaving the chamber, enjoying that she was able to help her dragon, Sadie burst out laughing as Orion pointed and in mock exasperation asked, "Did you have to kill them all? I heard someone mention something called Anger Management classes. Should we get you enrolled?"

Taking a step back, she played along by slamming her fists onto her hips and asking, "If the roles were reversed, you would have done the same thing. Don't even try to deny it."

Throwing his hands in the air in surrender, Orion laughed out loud. "Touché, *mo stór*. Touché."

124

Burning the bodies on their way toward the steps out of the underground compound, the couple let the ashes of the dead blow into the foliage to serve as fertilizer. Sadie said, "Pretty much what they deserve," while blowing warm air at the debris to help clear it away all the quicker.

Reaching the steel staircase, Orion stopped and turned on his good leg, looking back at all that Karura had built. "I believe we should leave this here. We are the only ones who know of its existence." He looked up at her and narrowed his eyes as he thought for a second then added, "It may just come in handy. What do you think?"

"I agree." She looked back as well, remembering her trek to save Orion. "I am sure my sisters would love to check it all out. Tinsley and Daphne, who you will meet in just a bit, and Phryne have learned quite a bit about electronics and computers in the past couple of years. Maybe we can turn this into something worthwhile. Do some good with what was meant to harm and hurt."

Wrapping his arm around her waist, Orion pulled her close and grinning from ear-to-ear, said, "Well, I have been locked away for over a century, so I will leave anything and everything technical to your sisters."

"I have not been locked away and I still leave everything technical to them. Just once I touched what the girls call a cell phone and it made so much noise, I swore never to go near it again." Sadie snickered.

"A cell phone?" Orion asked in amazement. "I have so very much to learn."

"Yes, but that will come later." Sadie nodded. "Now, enough stalling. Let's get you out of this hole and tend to your wounds."

Attempting to take charge as she always did, Sadie moved closer and tried to wrap her arm around Orion's waist at the precise moment he tried to do the same thing to her. Immediately correcting, the dragoness raised her arm to his shoulders, only to once again have her limbs tangled with her mate's. Two more tries and more bumping of arms had the couple laughing until tears ran down their faces.

Stepping back, Sadie got control of her giggles and said, "Okay, look, you need to stand still and let me get my arms around your waist. That way you can lean most of your weight onto me and keep it off that leg." She pointed to his still oozing wounds. "Once we get topside, Pearl will be able to help you and your dragon get the rest of the silver out of your system and you'll be good as new."

Orion was already shaking his head before she even finished speaking. "No." The one word hung between them. "I should be the one carrying you out of this hellhole. It is bad enough that I was captured and you had to free me, but this is simply too much. I am the male. It is my duty."

Staring at her mate, truly looking at the strong, defiant Alpha male the Universe had made just for her, Sadie wasn't sure if she should laugh at him or yell. Taking a moment to get her thoughts in order, the dragoness finally closed the distance, laid her hand on his shoulder, and looked deep into his turbulent cobalt eyes.

Running her fingertips along the strong line of his jaw, she smiled, "There is no denying that you are all male." She waggled her eyebrows to lighten his disposition. Her smile widened when he grinned just a bit. "But we are in this together." She dug her nails through his goatee, watching her mate's pupils dilate as she continued, "Look, I tried to fight it, deny it, and run away from it, but I finally had to accept the fact that you are my mate. We are destined to be." She let the hand that was touching his face fall to his other shoulder and leveled her gaze. "But if this is to work, we have to be a team. I am dragon. I am a princess. I have been trained to lead a clan since I took my first breath."

Orion slowly nodded as she went on, "We have to be true partners. You *cannot* treat me like a little *vibria* just learning to

127

flap her wings. I fight beside you, sword in hand, slaying our enemies just as you will do, or we end this now. We rule our clan *together*. We make all decisions as one. And if we disagree, which I have no doubt we will, *often*," she chuckled, "we compromise. We are…"

Orion's lips slammed to hers. All thought, not to mention her words, were obliterated as he opened not only his mind, but also his heart and soul completely to her. She felt the strength of his commitment combined with the love and adoration both man and dragon had for her and her dragoness growing by leaps and bounds. But most of all, she saw and felt his respect and unconditional belief in her and all that she stood for. And it was then Sadie knew beyond all doubt that this man, this dragon, would not only be her partner but support her in *all things*…just as she would do for him.

Pulling back from their kiss, breathless and starry-eyed, Sadie grinned. "Does that mean you agree?"

Barking with laughter as he hugged her close, she felt the rumble of her mate's chest as he readily agreed, "Oh yes, Sadie, my love, I concur most wholeheartedly." Leaning back, he waited until she looked up at him and then added, "And when those old insecurities and doubts come calling, because they will, trust someone who knows, all you have to do is tell me and I will be there to reassure you, love you, and remind you that there is no one in all the world who loves and adores you as I do."

Holding back her tears of joy, Sadie could only nod. Pulling back, she cleared her throat, blew out a breath, and quietly murmured, "Thank you and…" She looked back up only to find him staring down at her. Taking yet another deep breath, she whispered the words that scared her most of all. "And I love you."

Orion's hands gently cupped her cheek and it was then she saw the unshed tears in his eyes as he smiled sweetly and said, "Oh, Sadie, my beautiful, *beautiful* dragoness, I love you more than I ever dreamed possible." Laying his lips to hers, the couple confirmed with their kiss the true depth of their love and commitment.

Several long, glorious moments later, Sadie ended their kiss with a happy sigh and patting Orion's shoulder, said, "Okay, we have put this off long enough. Lean on me and let's get out of this horrible hole in the ground."

"Lead on, my princess, lead on."

It took almost ten minutes for Sadie to help Orion out of Karura's lair. Several times along their slow journey up those seventy-five steps, she thought about just picking him up and carrying him out, but then realized what a tremendous disrespect that would be to her mate. Not to mention that if he did that to her, she would be ready to kill him. So, she walked beside him, supported him when he needed, and stood by and let him do it on his own when he needed that too, just as she had said she would do. It was a big step for the dragoness and one that filled her with more joy than she had ever known.

Breathing in the fresh, crisp air of a new day, their freedom and an enemy conquered, the couple sat under the same tree where they had consummated their love less than a week before. Sitting between Orion's legs, wrapped in the warmth and security of his strong arms, the strong, steady beat of his heart matching hers where her back touched his chest, Sadie's eyes had just begun to get heavy when the sound of approaching footsteps had her jumping to her feet.

Grabbing her bow from where she'd hidden it before her descent to save her mate, the dragoness placed the arrow, pulled back her arm, and growled, "Show your face, intruder. Show your face *now* or you die."

Chapter Twelve

Struggling to his feet, Orion immediately sensed the appearance of one of his own. Slowly turning to Sadie, he laid his hand upon the shaft of her arrow and calmly said, "It is all right, my love." Then raising his voice so his brother could hear, the Shadow added with a chuckle, "I happen to know the decrepit old dragon approaching."

Barking with laughter so loud that Orion heard the Assassin before he saw him, Drago yelled, "If I am decrepit then you are ancient."

Seeing his old friend and Commander's face, the Shadow chuckled. "No truer words were ever spoken." Watching the man Orion had followed into more battles than he could ever remember with his arm around an attractive redhead whose blue eyes nearly brimmed with mischief, Orion had to admit Dragon MacLendon looked truly happy for the first time in their very, *very* long relationship.

"Orion McKendrick, I am pleased to introduce Alicia MacLendon." If possible, the Commander's smile widened when he added, "My mate."

Holding out his hand, the Shadow smiled, "I am very pleased to meet you, Alicia." Orion stepped back and put his arm around Sadie. "Drago and Alicia MacLendon, this is Sadie Ashford, the absolute love of my life."

The Assassin's brows furrowed as he asked, "As in Scathach Sorcha Ashford of the Ashford Dragons?"

"Yes, that's me," Sadie mumbled, her cheeks turning a beautiful shade of red.

"Excuse me for saying so, but we, as in all of dragon kin, thought you were dead." Drago smiled.

"Yeah, she gets that a lot." A voice Orion didn't recognize sounded behind him.

"The tales of her death were greatly exaggerated." Phryne laughed out loud, appearing beside he and Sadie alongside a tall, thin woman with whiskey eyes, an olive complexion, and light brown hair whom he immediately identified as a hippogriff.

These ladies have done a good job of staying hidden...

Smiling despite her discomfort, Sadie quickly explained, "Commander, these are two of my sisters, Phryne and Tinsley."

"Girls, this is Drago, Orion's Commander, and his mate, Alicia."

"Nice to meet you," Sadie's sisters answered in unison.

"You have been back less than a week and have found the lost princess of dragon kin, a Pegasus, and a Hippogriff? I swear, Shadow, only you," Drago's laughter rang in his head.

"And that is not all. Sadie's clan is made up of not only these three ladies, but also a thunderbird, a strix, a gargoyle, and a hoopoe. They have…"

"Is my mate telling all my secrets already?" Sadie chuckled, bursting in on Orion's conversation with his Commander.

"I was just…"

"He was just answering my question," Drago cut off Orion to explain. "And I apologize, Your Highness. I am just so amazed that not only you are still alive, but also lady shifters from extinct, or nearly extinct races. It is truly a blessing that you all have survived."

"And they were raised by one of the revered Guardians," Orion added, full of pride.

Shaking her head with her cheeks once again pink from embarrassment, Sadie chuckled. "First of all, I haven't been Your Highness for over a century, so please, call me Sadie. And as for the rest, my sisters are very special women who suffered the loss of all they had ever known at a very young, just as I did. We have done the best with what we were given. The Guardian kept us safe, raised us well, and provided us with all we would ever need to make our own decision whether to reenter the world or stay on the outskirts when the time was right." She shrugged. "We decided to stay together. We are family." The dragoness looked at her clanmates. "And I cannot imagine my life without them."

"I completely understand," Drago nodded. "That is how I feel about Orion and the other lads." He hugged Alicia closer. "And Alicia's family, too." He smiled, "I want to assure you that your secret is safe with me."

Orion pulled Sadie close as she said, "I know things are about to change and," she looked up at him with love in her eyes, "I think it's going to be good for all of us."

Kissing her on the forehead and hugging her tight, Orion added, "But we will stay with her clan, if that is what she wants."

"Aye, lad," Drago quickly agreed. "We have all made the decision to stay with our mates." The Commander looked down at Alicia and for the first time, Orion understood the starry-eyed expression he saw on his Commander's face, had seen on all mated males' faces. For it matched the one he knew was on his own face every time he looked at Sadie. "I am just glad your mind speak is working again. I began to think we were going to have to have Brannoc or Lenn, one of the young ones you have yet to meet, put a tracker on your sorry hide."

The Assassin narrowed his eyes and lowered his voice, "Because if you run off again without a word, you might not have a sorry hide for anyone to find."

Laughing out loud, Orion gave a sloppy salute with his left hand and teased, "Aye sir, understood."

"Don't let him talk to you like that, Orion," Alicia swatted her mate's chest. "I keep telling him he needs to relax."

"The Commander relax? Now that, I have got to see," Orion joked, making the whole group laugh.

As the revelry died down, Sadie said, "Drago, Alicia, you are welcome to come back to the lair with us, but I need to get Orion to Pearl so she can look at the silver poisoning in his leg and foot."

"If you are sure you do not mind, we would love to." Drago nodded. "And Alicia is quite good with healing. She might be able to help, as well."

"It's really nothing."

The words were barely out of Orion's mouth before his mate was growling. "I can feel how much it hurts and can see the silver traveling through your system." She poked him in the chest and he knew she was trying to sound tough while trying not to smile. "So, you will let Pearl and Alicia look at your leg and you will not argue with me about it. Is that clear?"

Taking her by surprise, Orion kissed his lovely dragoness hard and fast and then smiled as he pulled away, leaving her breathless. "As you wish, my love. Always, as you wish."

Looking at Drago, she asked with a snicker, "Was he always this incorrigible?"

"Most times worse." The Assassin laughed.

"Heavens help you, Commander. How did you ever survive?"

"Hey! Now!" Orion cried in mock outrage, making the whole group erupt in laughter again.

"All right, you heard the princess," Drago took control in his 'always a commander, never a foot soldier' way. "Let's get the Shadow to the lair."

"The Shadow?" Sadie asked with the most adorably perplexed look on her face the Guardsman just had to give her another quick kiss.

"Yes, mo ghrá. I have a special ability." He lowered his voice and waggled his eyebrows. *"One I will share with you...later."*

"All right, Casanova," she chuckled, *"I'll look forward to your big reveal."*

Walking to the home of the Ladies of the Sky was more enjoyable than it should have been and Orion chalked it all up to being snuggled up close to Sadie every step of the way. He could feel his dragon working hard to push all the silver from his system and heal his wounds, as well as his lovely mate's dragon doing the same. Nonetheless, he held tight to his princess.

Arriving at her lair was like walking through The Looking Glass. The Guardian had placed all manner of wards and mysticism that hid, disguised, and made finding it impossible for all but the seven ladies to whom it belonged. He had known the Guardian possessed the strength of the ages but was still shocked that it remained so long after her death.

Walking through the veil of trees and magic, Orion was awestruck by the small village the women had created. He smiled as the feeling of welcome and home filled not only his heart, but also that of his dragon.

"What is that smile for?" Sadie asked, steering him toward the two-story white cottage with black shutters and a red door.

The Guardsman took in the neatly manicured front yard, butterflies and bees flitting from one beautiful blossom to another in her garden, and the way it simply personified the woman he had fallen in love with as he answered, "I was just thinking this looks like a good place to live for a century or two. What do you think?"

Sadie's eyes grew as big as saucers. She stopped walking and turned completely toward him, placing both hands on his chest. "Are you serious?"

"Didn't you hear what the Commander said? We all can choose where we live and, my love," he cupped her cheek, "I choose you. Every time without fail, Sadie Ashford, I choose you." Without another thought, Orion laid his lips to hers, reaffirming with his kiss the words he had just spoken.

"All right, all right, enough of this kissy face stuff." Pearl walked up behind them with a tall blonde he identified as a gargoyle and a woman who looked exactly like Snow White from the fairy tales he'd heard the little vibrias reading what seemed like a lifetime ago, who he immediately knew was one, probably the last, of the legendary Hoopoe.

"Girls," Sadie smiled, "this is my," she took a deep breath, nodded, and said, "my mate, Orion." Then she turned to the Commander and his mate. "And this is Drago and Alicia, some of Orion's family."

The dragoness then introduced her family. "Pearl, you know." She patted Orion's chest. "The other two are Lauren," she pointed to the tall blonde. "And the one who is all smiles and looks like she is about to burst with excitement is Daphne. There is nothing in the world she likes more than a good love story." Sadie looked back and Orion and winked. "So, get ready. She will be asking for the details of our meeting."

Bursting out laughing, Phryne cackled, "Yeah, I wanna be there when Orion explains to Daphne about how you two met. Oh, puh-lease, let me be there."

Failing miserably at containing his laughter, Orion still tried to be stern when he said, "And that's about enough out of you, Miss Phryne." But the group still laughed all the way into Sadie's home with the Pegasus telling him to 'watch his back' because she had always wanted a brother to pick on.

It took Alicia and Pearl, with the consummate help of his dragon, a few hours to flush the remaining silver from his system and get all his wounds closed to the point that they were only raised red lines all over his arms, legs, and torso. His head wounds had thankfully healed very quickly, making the Strix comment, "Wow, your dragon has great healing powers. You are a very lucky man."

"Indeed I am."

The Guardsman had just uttered the words when Sadie walked into the room fresh from a shower, her hair hanging in long waves around her gorgeous face. Unable to hold back, Orion held up one hand while patting the bed beside him and smiled coyly, "Come and sit with me, *mo stór*."

"And that is my cue to find Drago," Alicia snickered, standing and heading for the door.

"I am right with you," Pearl chuckled, adding, "You two behave yourselves. He's not completely healed yet," over her shoulder as she shut the door.

Holding her hand, Orion searched for the perfect words for what he was about to propose but when they failed, he simply spoke from his heart. Looking into her expressive brown eyes, the Guardsman smiled. "Fate has brought us together and I could not be happier. I truly never thought I would have a mate. Not after the years of imprisonment and time away from our kin. But, I now see that it is true...the Universe does not make mistakes."

He kissed the back of her hand, taking a moment to breathe before continuing, "We never know what is going to happen. I am a Guardsman. You are a princess. We are both warriors. Look at all we have overcome to be in this place, at this time...together."

Taking a deep breath, Orion rushed on, "And because of that, I do not want to wait one more week, one more day, one more hour, to be your mate."

"But you are my mate," Sadie interjected, looking a bit confused.

"Yes, *mo chroí*, I most assuredly am, and I do not care if we are covered in the blood of our enemies, sitting on the front porch in rocking chairs, or standing before the Dragon Kings themselves, you, Scathach Sorcha Ashford, Rightful Leader of the Ashford Dragons, will be my mate, both officially and properly in the way of our ancestors, before we lay down beside one another on this night."

Orion watched a myriad of emotions cross her lovely face before his mate smiled so sweetly and brightly it almost broke his heart and uttered the words he'd been longing to hear since he'd first laid eyes on her. "Yes, by all the Heavens and my birthright, yes, Orion McKendrick, it would be my honor to officially and properly be your mate."

Pulling Sadie to his chest, Orion crushed his lips to hers and let the words, *"No happier man or dragon was there ever in the world,"* float from his thoughts to hers.

Chapter Thirteen

"Because I am not an Elder or a Guardian, or even a dragon," Pearl laughed, "I asked Sadie and Orion to each say something from their hearts, to vow to one another before all of us, the Universe, the Goddess of all, Fate, Destiny, and all the Deities of our very diverse kin, that they are committed to one another as true mates and will love one another, forsaking all others, here on Earth and in the Heavens beyond that."

"Because she is our leader and the first of our clan to find her mate, we are setting precedence today. I believe, as we all do, that because of our differences we are made stronger. Not ever have such unique and special individuals formed a family, a true bond of kinship, that will last until the end of time." She looked to Orion and then to Sadie before continuing, "And today we welcome the beginning of a new era, the expansion of our family. May we all embrace this change as our clan grows in numbers, strength, and love."

"Now, it is my honor to hush up and let the couple speak from their hearts, as I believe our great Universe always intended."

As Pearl stepped back, Sadie looked up at Orion and couldn't help but smile. All cleaned up with his goatee trimmed and his hair almost tamed in a que at the back of his head, he looked so dashing that the princess almost forgot what she wanted to say. Taking a deep breath before she truly did forget, Sadie started, "Orion, dragon of my heart, I pledge my love to you and everything that I am or will ever be. My first thought of every day will be of you. I will wait to see your face as every minute passes and rejoice when you are in my arms again. I cannot wait to spend eternity beside you, in love. You, and only you, will I honor above all others. My love, the greatest love a woman can have for her mate, is never ending and will remain so forevermore, just as I will remain by your side. This is my vow to you, my mate, my love, *grá mo chroí.*"

Watching as the blue of Orion's eyes intensified, Sadie's heart felt as if it might burst when he finally began to speak. "Sadie, *mo ghrá*, you honor me with your words, your love, and all that you are. I am the luckiest, happiest, most content dragon in all the land to have one such as you as the light to my darkness, the other and better half of my soul, and the one woman in all the world created to stand with me no matter what Fate, Destiny, or any other have in store for us."

"I vow by all the love in my heart, the desire in my soul, and the strength of both myself and my dragon, to always attempt to be a mate you are proud of. To honor you and your dragoness with my every thought, deed, and action. I will love you completely, wholly, and without restraint for all the days of my life and beyond. Do not ever change, for I respect you just as you are. You are my heart, my soul, my love, and my reason for being. Never shall we part. *Le grá go deo, gráim thú.*"

Sadie could barely breathe. Never had she felt so loved, so adored…so complete as she did in that moment, under the stars pledging her love to the man she knew beyond all doubt she was meant to love. Pearl's words pulled the princess from her thoughts as the Strix said, "So, I will ask, are there any among you who object to this union? If so, you must speak now."

When Pearl's question was met with silence, she smiled at Sadie while putting her hand on the dragoness' shoulder and lovingly murmured, "I love you, my sister. May you find all the happiness and more that you deserve." Then to their family, she spoke up, "I am happier than I can tell you to present the mated couple of Scathach Sorcha Ashford and Orion McKendrick. May the Universe shine its everlasting light on their love and may it bloom and grow and bless their children, their children's children, and so on until the end of time." She winked at Orion, "Now, kiss my sister like you love her and make it real. This one is for all the marbles."

Sadie met Orion in a clash of fiery passion and unending love that seemed to fill not only her heart and soul, but every fiber of her being with utter bliss. Kissing her mate like he was the very air she breathed, all the dragoness could think of was consummating their union. However, the chuckles of her sisters and the clearing of Drago's throat had her reluctantly ending their embrace.

Turning in her mate's arms, the dragoness looked out on her family, both the ones she had always known and those she looked forward to becoming closer to, and beamed. "Thank you so much for sharing in the happiest, most perfect event in my life. I cannot wait for what is to come."

She chuckled as Orion kissed her neck, trying to distract her with not only his teasing, but also the wonderfully wicked thoughts he was letting flow from his mind to hers. Clearing her throat, the dragoness tried to focus as she said, "Tomorrow, we shall celebrate with a feast. Sleep well. May you have lovely dreams and know that I love each and every one of you to the bottom of my very soul."

Sadie had barely spoken the last words when Orion scooped her up in his arms and raced across the meadow to her home with the laughter of their loved ones ringing in her ears. Kicking open the door, he barely had it closed before he raced up the stairs into her room and she was sliding down his body.

Unable to form a single coherent thought, Sadie threw herself into Orion's arms, kissing him with every ounce of strength in her body. Pulling open his shirt, she slid her hands under the soft cotton, shoving it off his shoulders and down his back until it dropped to the floor. Her fingers danced over his amazing body. Electrical currents arched between them. Sparks raced throughout her body, landing deep in her womb and igniting a blaze only Orion could quench.

Sliding down his body, Sadie kissed, tasted, and teased. She memorized every inch of the man the Universe had made for her, knowing she would spend eternity thinking of new, inventive ways to show him how very much he meant to her. Paying special attention to the multitude of scars and glyphs left from his decades of torture, the dragoness kissed the damaged skin, pouring unconditional love and immense adoration into their bond.

Over his shoulder, she came eye to eye with the marking representing his dragon. She knew the beast's massive wings and body covered her mate's back but at that moment, Sadie outlined the beast's ridged brow and the long, curved battle horns upon his head with the tip of her finger, chuckling as goose bumps rose all over Orion's wonderfully muscled chest.

Placing butterfly kisses on the dragon's snout, she smiled against her mate's heated skin as he hissed and held his breath with each caress. Her hand massaged the muscles of his six-pack, working her way toward the waistband of his pants while her lips continued to nip and taste his delectable flesh. Sadie simply could not get enough of Orion and reveled in each of his groans as her fingers teased his straining cock through the worn cotton of his jeans.

Pulling her hands to his belt, she slid the leather through the loops and smiled as the buckle clattered against the tiled floor. Unbuttoning his pants, Sadie let her hand follow the trail of dark hair, sighing when her fingers stretched to cover the girth of his erection. Her heart sped as he throbbed against her palm. Working her fist up and down several times, loving the catch in Orion's breath, she rubbed her thumb through the drop of wetness that had already gathered at the tip, spreading the proof of his excitement all over his swollen head. Orion's fists clenched at his sides and in her mind, he growled, "*Sadie,* mo banphrionsa, mo bhanríon *I...lo...love you.*"

"*And I love you,* mo chroí, mo rí," she whispered in return, rubbing her thumb along the thick pulsing vein on the underside of his cock.

Orion rolled his hips, dragging his cock in and out of her clenched fist as his breathing became more erratic, his movements more frantic, his thoughts more chaotic. Looking up, she watched the pulse in his neck pound a heavy beat, loving that she could drive her mate as wild as he drove her.

Groaning loudly, Orion's head fell back and his fists beat against his tensed thighs, signaling how close to losing control he truly was. Working her fist up and down his generous length, she used her free hand to shove his jeans to the floor. As he kicked them out of the way, she placed her free hand on his thigh and leaned forward, taking as much of his erection into her mouth as she could. His essence exploded on her tongue.

Slowly and deliberately, she let him slide from her mouth, only to tease the slit at the tip with her tongue. Orion's hands flew to her head and tangled in her hair. Tension built in his fingers as he gently massaged her scalp. The muscles in his powerful legs quivered against her hands as the need to move his hips grew.

Longing to see her dragon utterly lost in the throes of passion, she sucked him back into her mouth until the tip of his cock touched the back of her throat then hollowed her cheeks and swallowed as deliberately as she could. The low, rumbling groan from Orion's lips nearly rattled the windows. His hands shifted to her shoulders and his hips drew back, attempting to pull his erection from her mouth.

Sliding her hand to the back of his thigh, she held tight and whispered, *"Please, Orion, please let me love you."*

He immediately stopped resisting with a barely intelligible groan, and even stronger feelings of love and commitment flowed between them, spurring the dragoness on. Sliding her lips over him, Sadie once again was using her free hand to tenderly tease and massage his balls.

A grumble that started low in his throat turned to a growl and ended up as a roar of her name. "Sadie…oh gods, Sadie… *Beidh mé grá duít go geo!"*

Not wanting to stop loving her mate, the dragoness hummed her agreement to his beautiful words. The vibrations from her response were a happy accident that caused him to groan louder and longer and for her to smile, making a note to remember how much he liked that one simple move.

Lost to their passion, Orion attempted to pull from her mouth with as much force as Sadie tried to keep him there. The resulting motion was a give and take, in and out, where the couple met one another stroke for stroke. The faster they went, the harder it became for her mate to breathe, his balls tightening in her hand.

Wanting to taste all that he was, Sadie quickened their pace, using her enhanced speed to move him in and out of her mouth faster and faster until Orion roared her name. Sadie swallowed every drop of his warm, wet essence, continuing to work him across her lips until his breathing slowed and his muscles relaxed.

Removing her hand from the back of his thigh, Orion rolled his hips until he fell from her lips and then knelt before her. Placing his hands on her waist, her dragon looked at her with so much love, Sadie didn't even try to stop the tears that wet her cheeks. Smiling a smile the dragoness knew was only for her, Orion said, "Thank you for your love, your strength, and for not running anymore. Without you, Sadie Ashford McKendrick, I am just an old dragon, lost and alone in a world he doesn't understand."

Leaning forward, he placed a kiss on her forehead, then one on each cheek, then one on each side of her mouth before working his way all the way down her throat. His journey continued to the neckline of the light blue dress her sisters had picked out for her. Every inch of her décolletage knew his attention, while his hands slowly worked down the zipper at her back. Sadie sighed as her dress floated to the floor, leaving her naked but for her white silk panties.

In one fluid motion, Orion pulled her to her feet. She could feel his eyes caressing every part of her body from the tip of her toes to her long flowing hair she had left down as he had requested. Sadie felt her nipples harden and the dampness of her arousal wet the inside of her thigh.

"You are the most perfect woman, dragon, princess, leader…person, I have ever known. I am humbled to be by your side and I will spend eternity showing you exactly how much you mean to me. I belong to no other. You own me, body, mind and soul," he reverently whispered before crushing his lips to hers.

Laying them back on the bed while whispering words of love and devotion into her mind, Orion kissed and tasted until Sadie knew she would never be able to live without his touch. They were irrevocably intertwined for all time…one in heart, one in mind, one in body, and one in soul.

The sensual overload was nothing short of miraculous. His hands on her body, their shared feelings, his voice in her mind, and their hearts beating as one, drove the dragoness insane with desire. His fingers slid under the silk on her hip and one tug later, she was completely naked and utterly at his mercy.

Ladies of the Sky

Sadie lifted her hips, trying to force his wandering hands where she ached the most, but Orion merely chuckled and placed his hand atop her mound, sliding his thumb back and forth, teasing her excited clit. Goose bumps raised all over her body. The dragoness growled her frustration through gritted teeth, using only his name, "Please…please *mo ghra'*, please, Orion love me."

She could hear the smile in his voice as he answered, "Oh yes, *mo bhanríon*, I will love you now and forever more."

His body moved against hers and the contact only heightened her soaring arousal. Looking down her body, she saw him kneeling between her legs. Their eyes met, held Sadie captive, unable to do anything but look into the eyes of the man that owned her as no other ever had or would.

Placing his hands under her ass, he pulled her closer. The head of his cock touched her wet curls, causing her hips to lift of their own accord. Sadie sighed as Orion slid between her outer lips and bumped her clit. She struggled to move her hips forward. Tried with all her might to push him farther inside. They gasped in unison at the sensations her movements caused. Staring into one another's souls, acknowledging their unbreakable bond, the couple began to move in unison.

His hard, throbbing cock invaded her wet, warm pussy, stretching her, owning her, stopping only when he could go no farther. The feeling of utter bliss filled both dragons. The words, *a union blessed by the Universe Herself*, floated through Sadie's mind in the Guardian's voice.

Delighting in the feeling of her womb contracting around Orion's throbbing erection, they paused, letting the flood of emotion wash over them both. The uninhibited passion flowing between them heightened the couple's desire. Their hearts beat as one. Their bodies moved as one. They *were* one, for all time.

Orion's eyes looked down her body, leaving a scorching trail of unbridled passion in their wake. "Look at us, *mo maité'*. Perfectly joined together..." His words trailed off in reverence.

At just a glimpse of their joined bodies, Sadie's need compounded. Her hips moved with renewed vigor. The sight of him gliding in and out of her was the most beautiful thing she'd ever seen. Orion immediately responded, driving in and out of her, rolling his hips with every thrust. The tip of his cock rubbed against the bundle of nerves at the top of her channel as he bumped her swollen nub on every stroke.

Unable to do anything but feel, Sadie held tight to the love and devotion she felt for her dragon and reached for his hands. Their fingers intertwined as she screamed her release to the

Heavens a split second before Orion roared his at precisely the moment the dragoness felt a sting on the left side of her neck. She knew at once it was just as she'd been told when she was younger, *'And the Universe shall mark you both, as mates, as one under Her divine providence, for all to see.'*

Slowly returning to earth, she reveled in the feel of Orion moving ever so slowly in and out of her with their hands still clasped. She grinned at his voice, rough from their lovemaking, when he asked, "Hello, *mo ghrá*, have you returned to me?"

Sadie didn't attempt to hide her pleasure as she purred, "As I always will, *mo chroi'*, as I always will." Touching her neck at the same time that she saw the mark of double dragon wings on Orion's neck, the dragoness added, "And we have been marked. Yet another blessing from the Universe."

Pulling himself from her, Orion crawled up Sadie's body, kissed her soundly, and laid on his side facing her. She felt his hand slip under her pillow and rolled to face him. "What are you up to?" Sadie asked.

Handing her a small velvet bag, Orion smiled, "Open it and see."

Holding her breath, Sadie carefully loosened the string, tipped the bag, and gasped when the most perfect Opal ring with

154

spectacular fire set in an intricate gold setting fell into her hand. The oval cut gem was surrounded by glittering diamonds and the Claddagh signs sat under the setting on both sides of the band with diamonds set in the gold that would go all the way around her finger.

Orion took the ring from her palm and held her left hand in his. Looking deep into her eyes, he promised, "You are mine and I am yours, heart to heart, hand to hand, never shall we part. *Is brae liom tú.*" Then he slid the ring on her finger.

"Where did you...How did you?" Sadie was shocked, stuttering and more in love than she ever could have imagined.

Laughing, Orion explained, "Drago's nephew, Rayne, has been holding onto all our most sacred belongs that the Elders of our clans kept after our disappearance. The Commander carries them with him at all times, for occasions such as this." He kissed her quickly then added. "It was my grandmother's. She was mated to Orran, one of the original Dragon Kings, who I am loosely named after and inherited this ability from."

The air filled with her mate's magic combined with that of his dragon's as Orion completely disappeared from sight while finishing his thought aloud. "It was her dying wish that my mate wear the ring given to her by her one true mate and that we share the bountiful love and blessed life that they had."

It was weird to hear his voice and feel his touch but not be able to see him. So, using her preternatural sight, Sadie was able to barely make out a light outline of the man she loved, seeing exactly how he had earned the nickname 'The Shadow'. "That is amazing," she beamed, even more in awe of the man the Universe had made for her.

"And this ring is simply," the tears began to fall again as she blubbered, "Oh, Orion," not even caring that she prided herself on never crying and was doing it for the second time in the same day. "And how appropriate that the opal is the sacred stone of the Ashford Dragons. You are absolutely amazing. I love you."

"And you," he pulled her closer, "are nothing less than absolute perfection, my Queen."

"Queen is it, now?" Sadie chuckled, cuddling closer to the man she knew she could love forever.

"Oh yes, you are most assuredly the Queen of this castle, Mrs. Sadie Ashford McKendrick," he chuckled. "Forever may you reign," he added before pulling her even closer and laying his lips to hers.

"You are the best thing that has ever or will ever happen to me. I love you with every scale on this old dragon's hide."

The words floated through her mind as their kiss deepened and Sadie could only answer, *"And the dragon queen and her king lived happily ever after…"*

THE END

PHRYNE'S FIGHT

Coming July 2017

Book #2 in the Ladies of Sky Series

After a hundred and some years on Earth, Phryne Fairchild has just learned the definition of a really bad day.

It was bad enough that she found herself trapped in animal form but now, she's lost the ability to call forth her wings, is unable to speak telepathically with her sisters...and was just rustled like a pack mule into the back of a stinky old horse trailer with five wild stallions. Bad just became worse and is heading towards the makings of her worst nightmare. What's a Pegasus to do with no magic and no wings?

Following up on a lead concerning the wild horse disappearances, Det. Jed Harrison finds evidence of an enemy as old as time. One that brings death and destruction not only to the Native Americans, but to all in Its path. As the trail grows cold, Jed is faced with another, even harsher reality, the scent of a long-lost breed, one that brings hope and vitality to not only his people but also the stallion with whom he shares his soul. Can he beat the ticking clock to save not only his tribe but also the mate of his heart?

With the power of the Great Spirit and the strength of the Universe, one majestic Stallion will move Heaven and Earth to have the Destiny designed for him by Fate, but will it be enough?

Join the journey of the Ladies of the Sky…Once You Take Flight, the World Will Never Look the Same Again.

HER DRAGON TO SLAY

Check Out the One that Started It All for the Dragon Guard

Dragon Guard Book #1

FREE ON ALL RETAILERS

Sassy and stubborn have gotten Kyndel through everything life had to throw at her. Will her moxie help when destiny falls at her feet?

Hundreds of years of loyalty to Dragon Guard have made Rayne a fearless leader. When the long-foretold pull of his mate rocks the Commander's world to its core will he be able to save her from his enemies in time?

The chemistry between this strong-willed curvy girl and fierce warrior makes all the difference in the world where nothing is as it seems. The existence of an ancient race of honor-clad, tradition-bound protectors might be hard to accept but now the dead are coming back to life and holding a knife to her neck.

Can these fated mates defeat their greatest enemies and get their happily ever after?
Fate Will Not Be Denied!!

Available at all retailers. Grab your copy today!

OUT OF THE ASHES

Guardians of the Zodiac, Book #1

A Zodiac Shifters Paranormal Romance

AVAILABLE NOW

Meet the Guardian of the Zodiac and introducing the Dragon Guard of the Sea!

Lost and thought dead, these mighty dragons arise from the depths to not only help to save all mankind but reunite with others of their kind.

The mission is simple – get into the enemy camp, free the humans, return the demons to Hell and return home the victor. For a Daughter of Poseidon and her constant companion, Drákon – a centuries old water dragon, that's called a good day at work.

Everything is going as planned. Una, eldest daughter and Guardian of Pisces, has checked one and two off her list, and is headed to three when things get complicated. Brody Mason bows at her feet, pledging his allegiance to not only her but also, the gods and the Light. As a show of loyalty, he promises to take her to the portal from Hell and with his own blood help her close the door on the Underworld. This one act will rid the world of evil forever. There's only one problem…he's a Hellhound.

Ladies of the Sky

It doesn't matter that Drákon doesn't believe him, fearing it yet another trick of Hades to deter them from their mission or that there's fire in his eyes and the smell of brimstone on his olive skin, she can feel the truth in his words. It also doesn't hurt that with just one glance he sets her heart ablaze and her pulse racing. Not that this is about love or lust, it is all about saving the Earth, protecting the humans, defeating her uncle's evil...or is it?

One leap of faith leads Una and Brody on a race against time and facing the fight of their lives. Hiding from Poseidon, Hades and an army of Guardians led by her sister, Zoe, this couple may have the best intentions but in the end, isn't that what paves the road to Hell?

Available at all retailers. Grab your copy today!

MARROK: A Wolf's Hunger by Julia Mills

Book #3 in AK Michaels' Bestselling Multi-Author

Series – A Wolf's Hunger

Insatiable Hunger…

Desire Beyond Compare…

An Alpha on the hunt for his fated mate…

Marrok Kilbride has faced insurmountable odds - returned from the dead, killed those threatening his pack and even watched his sister find the mate of her heart but never has he experienced anything like the voracious, mindless hunger dogging his every step, and it all started with…*her*.

The fire racing through his veins cannot be extinguished. His wolf cannot be tamed. Both man and beast must have his mate…or die trying.

Sleepless nights, hallucinations, and the inability to keep his wolf contained all are part of the Legendary Hunger, a myth the old ones speak of, a fable come to life to not only torment but taunt and terrorize this Alpha to the point of sneaking onto Pride Lands and taking what he knows to be his.

But she's gone…kidnapped…taken from under his nose and hidden away…

The hunt is on. There's no time to waste. He will find her and make her his, God help anyone who gets in his way.

This isn't about Fate or Destiny… This is A Wolf's Hunger, It Cannot Be Stopped.

Available on Amazon and with Kindle Unlimited!

ACHILLES ~ Book 3 in the Kings of the Blood Series

Available Now!

A scream in the night. A panicked call for help. There's no time to think. The rules be damned.

A fate worse than death. Buried alive…lost…alone… A centuries old secret her only hope. May the gods be on her side.

This one's about more than brotherhood.

Save the girl…save the Kings.

Available on Amazon and with Kindle Unlimited!

LOLA: A 'Not-Quite' Witchy Love Story

Part of the Magic & Mayhem Kindle World

Available Now!

The Asscrack Gang and I are about to get busy!

Being single in a world where everything is thorn-covered roses and bags of bloody bones sucks! Heidi's got Hunter, Bert's got Luci…hell, even Lucifer's got Trixie and then there's me, the sexiest alter ego this side of Purgatory… stuck inside a Hellhound who's happier than a zombie at the body farm in her new wedded bliss. Sure, Heidi and her Hunkie Hellhound hump like rabbits getting ready for Easter but even that's gotten boring. I need to get out, see the Underworld, sow my wild oats. I mean, a girl's gotta get hers while the gettin's good, am I right?

It's taken six long months of bitchin'… I mean persuading, but Heidi's finally agreed to let me have a body of my own. So, it's back into the Lady Bug Express and off to West Virginia, but this time we're avoiding the crazy Aunties and heading straight for Asscrack. Zelda, the next Baba Yaga and Almighty Shifter Wanker has agreed to help. She plans to yank me outta Heidi and shove me into a fresh new body before the next full moon. Then it's bingo bango, Lola's gonna get her groove on.

It looks like I might even end up with some powers, seems Katie, the chickie whose skin will now be mine, was a witch before she hocused when she should have pocused. I might have to sidestep her sisters and hideout from some vamps but it'll all be worth it. Imagine the possibilities… me with magic. I'm positively giddy at the idea.

The plan is flawless. I mean, come on, what could go wrong?

Available on Amazon!

About Julia

Hey Y'all! I'm Julia Mills the New York Times and USA Today Bestselling Author of the Dragon Guard Series. I without a doubt admit to being a sarcastic, southern woman who would rather spend all day laughing than a minute crying. Living with my two most amazing daughters and a menagerie of animals, keeps me busy but I love telling a good story. Now, that I've decided to write the stories running through my brain, life is just a blast!

My beliefs are simple. A good book along with shoes, makeup, and purses will never let a girl down and no hero ever written will compare to my real-life hero, my dad! I'm a sucker for a happy ending and alpha men make me swoon.

I'm still working on my story but I promise it will contain as much love and laughter as I can pack into it! Now, go out there and create your own story!!! Dare to Dream! Have the Strength to Try EVERYTHING! Never Look Back!

I ABSOLUTELY adore stalkers so look me up on Facebook – Julia Mills, Author and sign up for my newsletter at www.JuliaMillsAuthor.com Send me a message! I love talking to readers!

Thank you for reading my stories!!!

XOXO Julia

Proof

Made in the USA
Columbia, SC
01 June 2017